THE LULLABY TREE

The Lullaby Tree

Wim Coleman

A PLAY IN THREE ACTS

MADEIRA PRESS

CARRBORO, NC

Title page image: Aesop in a woodcut by an anonymous artist, from the 1489 Spanish edition of *Aesop's Fables (Fabulas de Esopo)*. The storyteller is shown surrounded by images and events from the *Life of Aesop* by Planudes. (From Wikimedia Commons.)

ISBN: 978-1-935178-49-1
Drama; Mythology; Visionary & Metaphysical

Drowned in Madeira wine, two flies began to recover life.
—*Benjamin Franklin*

"They had been drowned in Madeira wine…. Having heard it remarked that drowned flies were capable of being revived by the rays of the sun, I proposed making the experiment upon these…. In less than three hours, two of them by degrees began to recover life. They commenced by some convulsive motions in the thighs, and at length they raised themselves upon their legs, wiped their eyes with their fore feet, beat and brushed their wings with their hind feet, and soon after began to fly…. I should prefer to an ordinary death, the being immersed in a cask of Madeira wine, with a few friends … then to be recalled to life by the solar warmth of my dear country!"
—*The Autobiography of Benjamin Franklin*

for Pat and Monse

Jesus wept.
—John 11:35
(King James)

CONTENTS

PLAYWRIGHT'S NOTE x

CHARACTERS: xi

ACT I 1

ACT II 39

ACT III 109

Playwright's Note

The actor playing Aesop must be an outstanding mime and athlete as well as a capable speaker of both prose and verse. At one point, the stage directions call upon him to perform three extended handstands in rapid succession. Since this may be physically unreasonable, headstands are acceptable.

Because so much is said throughout the play about Aesop's extreme ugliness, it seems appropriately incongruous that he should be played by an exceptionally handsome actor; the performer's gender may not matter much.

Instrumental music is demanded at the beginning of Aesop's final verse monologue, followed by choral music a few stanzas later; of course, it would be ideal to have original music composed especially for the play. Lacking that, use the fifth movement of Mahler's Symphony No. 2 in C minor, beginning with the passage marked *"Sehr langsam und gedehnt."* With rehearsal, the actor playing Aesop can time the entrance of the chorus at the appropriate moment.

CHARACTERS:

APOLLO, *god of light, truth, and prophecy*
ILITHYIA, *goddess of childbirth*
MOTHER *of Aesop*
MIDWIFE
FATHER *of Aesop*
TWO STAGEHANDS, *non-speaking*
STEWARD *to a wealthy citizen of Samos*
AESOP, *teller of fables*
PRIESTESS *of the goddess Isis*
MNEMOSYNE, *goddess of memory and
    mother of the Nine Muses*
NINE MUSES:
    CLIO *(history)*
    URANIA *(astronomy)*
    MELPOMENE *(tragedy)*
    THALIA *(comedy)*
    TERPSICHORE *(dance)*
    CALLIOPE *(epic poetry)*
    ERATO *(love poetry)*
    POLYHYMNIA *(songs to the gods)*
    EUTERPE *(lyric poetry)*

SCENE:

The island of Samos; no time in particular

ACT 1

(Evening. A large tree stands upstage center, spreading its nearly barren branches wide and high. In front of the tree is a stone bench. The MOTHER *sits on the bench, holding a newborn baby in her arms. The* MIDWIFE *sits next to her, peering at the baby. Sitting on a branch of the tree, stage left, is the goddess* ILITHYIA. APOLLO *descends into the scene as a deus ex machina, alighting amid the branches, right. The mortal characters cannot hear the gods speak.* APOLLO *addresses the audience.)*

APOLLO.
> Ye mortals! Puny creatures of a day,
> Carcassed forth from dust and clay,
> Look and hear—witness our play!
> For I, Apollo, deign to say—

ILITHYIA *(to* APOLLO). Shhh. *(gesturing in front of her)* Fourth wall.

APOLLO. So we can't talk?

ILITHYIA. Between ourselves.

ILITHYIA. To nobody else?

ILITHYIA. Of course not. We're deities.

> *(Crossing his arms indignantly,* APOLLO *sits on a branch.)*

MOTHER. He's laughing.

MIDWIFE. So he is.

MOTHER. Have you ever heard one laugh so soon?

MIDWIFE. It's impossible.

MOTHER. A miracle!

MIDWIFE. Don't think too much of it.

MOTHER. But a miracle!

MIDWIFE. You just gave life. What's another miracle? They're cheap as figs today. I've seen many such days in my work. And I've seen days when there were no miracles at all.

APOLLO. And days when miracles were undone.

ILITHYIA. Oh, you mortals! There's only one miracle in all creation—that creation continues, on and on. The odds of each moment unfolding as it does—or unfolding *at all*— are simply preposterous. Reality itself is a never-ending coincidence, one far-fetched microsecond after another, and yet here you are, and here is the world. If you only knew, you'd live in fear every moment—fear that the one great miracle shall fail and all shall vanish, as all surely must.

MIDWIFE. How easy it was! And how well you both are! And how beautiful he is—with dimples of laughter and wisdom! And, oh, such eyes! The brightest in the world! And his fingers are so strong! Look, how they've found my thumb and wrapped themselves tightly around it. We must give thanks. I'll go make a sacrifice to Ilithyia.

APOLLO. Foolish midwife.

ILITHYIA. No sacrifices to me, thank you.

MOTHER. Stay with me.

ILITHYIA. Yes, stay with her.

MIDWIFE. Think of the next mother I help. Will the goddess be with me if I fail to give thanks now?

MOTHER. Ilithyia can wait.

MIDWIFE. Blasphemy!

ILITHYIA. I don't deserve thanks. I never do anything but watch. Let the mother thank herself—and you.

APOLLO. While there remains something to be thankful for.

ILITHYIA. What *are* you up to?

MOTHER. Stay just a little. Please.

MIDWIFE. Well.

MOTHER. Won't he stop laughing?

MIDWIFE. Should you want him to?

MOTHER. When will he sleep?

MIDWIFE. When he stops laughing.

MOTHER. Oh, but I'm tired.

MIDWIFE. Let me take him so you can nap.

MOTHER. No. I can't let go of him. Not yet. I'll have to soon enough. *(Laughing)* Oh, it's catching! What can be so funny, I wonder?

MIDWIFE. Laughing yourself, and you don't know?

MOTHER. I've got no idea.

MIDWIFE. The world, I suppose. That it's surrounded by air and not a vacuum. Go on and laugh. You deserve it.

MOTHER. But it hurts! My belly!

MIDWIFE. It's best to cry, then.

MOTHER. I'm crying too.

MIDWIFE. But you'll do yourself harm.

MOTHER *(laughing harder)*. I might even die.

MIDWIFE. This is serious.

MOTHER. It hurts more than giving birth.

MIDWIFE. You're giving birth to laughter.

MOTHER. Yes, I believe I am.

MIDWIFE. I've got no skill to help.

MOTHER. Then don't. I'll lose my life for something sublime. I'll fill the world with laughter!

MIDWIFE. There's too much of it already.

MOTHER. There can't be too much of it.

MIDWIFE. Too much mockery, anyway. Laughter is fleeting.

MOTHER. And my life isn't?

MIDWIFE. I'll not allow it. If he stops laughing, will you?

MOTHER. Oh, yes, but—

MIDWIFE. Then sing a lullaby.

MOTHER. I don't know one. You sing one.

MIDWIFE. No. It's bad luck.

MOTHER. Why?

MIDWIFE. A baby's first lullaby must be sung by his mother. Anyone else—it's worse than no good.

ILITHYIA. Superstitious fool.

MIDWIFE. Have you never heard a lullaby before?

MOTHER. I suppose. When I was little. Before I can remember.

MIDWIFE. Call upon Ilithyia. She'll bring you a song.

MOTHER. *You* call upon Ilithyia.

APOLLO *(to* ILITHYIA*)*. You're needed.

ILITHYIA. I'm never needed.

APOLLO. So you'll not give her a lullaby?

ILITHYIA. She'll find one in her heart.

MOTHER *(still laughing)*. Oh, a lullaby comes! Ilithyia grants
   your wish! A sublime joke, indeed!

MIDWIFE. No joke. A lullaby's as serious as death. Listen to
   Ilithyia.

MOTHER. But I can't stop laughing.

MIDWIFE. Breathe. Slowly. Listen. Sing.

   *(The MOTHER breathes slowly until her laughter
   wanes.)*

MOTHER *(singing)*.
   Budding fig,
   Baby fig,
   Clinging fast upon the twig,
   Daylight dims
   'Mid mother's limbs;
   Sleep snug so you'll grow ripe and big.

MIDWIFE. Yes, a song of a fig tree—just like the one we're
   sitting under. Keep on.

MOTHER *(singing)*.
   The breezes now
   Rock every bough;
   Fear not the why, fret not the how.
   Twilight weaves
   Throughout the leaves
   To smooth your worried little brow.

MIDWIFE. Ilithyia is kind.

MOTHER *(singing)*.
> Do not fear,
> Fig, my dear,
> When the little wasp comes near.
> Open wide;
> Let her inside;
> Give her a warm, safe place to hide.

MIDWIFE. It's working.

MOTHER *(singing)*.
> For she'll not sting;
> Instead, she'll bring
> A magic potion on her wing.
> You'll sprout another
> Fig-tree mother;
> So sleep, sweet fig, until the spring.

MIDWIFE. He's quiet now. And so are you. And just in time.
   I hear your husband coming. Give me the baby.

MOTHER. No, not yet!

MIDWIFE. You must.

MOTHER. But what if he … doesn't … ?

MIDWIFE. Don't be silly. What have you got to fear from
   the Raising? How on earth could he reject such a perfect
   creature?

MOTHER. But how can I be sure?

APOLLO.
> How, indeed? Ye mortals mere
> Are never wise but when you fear.
> This kind assurance I can give:
> However long you choose to live,
> This moment will haunt you with pain
> On and on and never wane.

ILITHYIA. You monster.

APOLLO. And what does that make you, immortal colleague?

ILITHYIA. I hate you.

APOLLO. I am the divine embodiment of sweetness and perfection. How better to honor me than to hate me?

MIDWIFE. Give me the baby.

MOTHER. I'm afraid.

MIDWIFE. Give me, give me! O tell me not of fear.

> (The MOTHER *reluctantly hands the baby to the* MIDWIFE, *who walks center stage, carefully wrapping the baby in its swaddling clothes.*)

MIDWIFE. And now, he must be covered completely, head to toe, so the father may give him a second birth to his own sight.

> (The MIDWIFE *sets the baby on the floor.*)

MIDWIFE. And now, I must set him here, upon cold stone—a foundling for a moment.

(The MIDWIFE *steps away from the baby to stand by the* MOTHER's *side.)*

MIDWIFE. And now—oh, this is key—we must be silent, both of us. Not the slightest murmur, no matter what unfolds. 'Twere better we weren't seen at all, weren't even here.

(A moment of silence; then the FATHER *enters. He glances fleetingly at the* MOTHER *and* MIDWIFE, *then hastily turns away as if he hadn't seen them. He kneels beside the covered, silent baby.)*

FATHER. New life—but are you mine? And shall you go on living? I once lay upon this same floor, as fresh to the world as you.

(The FATHER *touches the swaddling. The* MOTHER *can keep silent no longer.)*

MOTHER. It's a boy. A perfectly beautiful—

MIDWIFE. Hush!

(The FATHER *draws his hands away from the swaddling apprehensively.)*

FATHER. Boy—do you know who I am? A man of substance. In my younger days I was shoemaker. Today I'm a merchant of other cobbler's shoes. I've got a good bit of money, and I get more of it every day. But scant good it does me.

(The FATHER *takes a coin out of his purse.)*

FATHER. My coins shine brightly—they're too new. People

don't value a piece of gleaming silver. They like it old. They respect a man if his coins have idled in his palm a long time—most of all when they stink from the sweat of his father's palm.

I'd like to feed all my coins to the noisy geese, to pass through their gullets and guts and anuses and become stainèd with feignèd age. But that won't do. They're stamped with the smug face of our young archon, who has reigned in his puffed-up pride just these last three years. No, there's no tricking folks with falsely tarnished silver marked with a freshly foolish face. Better I fed myself to a goose.

Your grandfather was a slave. He did nothing but dig useless holes—the unwary were always falling into them. Oh, and he also filled them—to no better purpose, for people tripped over the mounds at night. And yet he hoarded enough coins to buy his freedom and this bit of land. His newborn son, my father, once lay upon this spot when it was naught but dirt, before these stones were laid.

My father was a butcher. For years he kept a wretched little stall that customers reached by climbing a ladder. For years he had but a few sparkling new coins—and daily he had to spend them, buying fresh meat to chop up and trade for more coins. But he squirreled away enough silver to build this house and put down these smooth stones upon which I once lay, upon which you lie now.

If I raise you up to live, what will you be? What will you do? 'Tis said a son's duty is to respect and obey his father, abidingly and always. Rubbish, I call it. It sets life going backward. I was fit to be my father's master, my father to be his father's master. I've long dreamed of a son who would be my master, before whom I must kneel, whom I must obey.

If I raise you up, make idleness your only work. Butchering meat and dealing in shoes are no better than digging and filling useless holes. Idleness alone gives silver its proper stench and tarnish. Idleness alone makes men respected and great. So be the idlest man on this island of Samos.

(Pause)

FATHER. Well. It's time. I'm supposed to say a rhyme now. Much as I've rehearsed it, I …

(Pause; the FATHER stares at the bundled baby.)

FATHER.
Now I see you on the ground,
I know not whether lost or found.
Let foolish hope not enter me—
Only one thought: Let be, let be.

(With trembling fingers, the FATHER reaches to pull the cloth from the baby's face.)

APOLLO.
Hold! Suspend! Await my spell!
Whatever's sweet, I'll turn to hell!

(The FATHER, MOTHER, and MIDWIFE all freeze; only APOLLO and ILITHYIA continue to move and speak.)

ILITHYIA. What will you do?

APOLLO. The baby's perfect, you say?

ILITHYIA. And so he'll remain.

APOLLO. No hope of that.

ILITHYIA. No sane soul asks for hope.

APOLLO. What do you want, then?

ILITHYIA. A touch of compassion.

APOLLO. You may have it.

ILITHYIA. Let this family live without your curse.

APOLLO. No.

ILITHYIA. Why not?

APOLLO. My role is to be cruel.

ILITHYIA. You promised compassion.

APOLLO. I give it.

ILITHYIA. Cruel and yet compassionate?

APOLLO. There's a difference? Silence, now. Your work is
      done, mine is to do.

> (APOLLO *floats from the tree branches down to the*
> *ground, standing beside the* FATHER *and the baby.*
> *Invisible to the still-frozen* FATHER, *he touches the*
> *bundle and speaks.*)

APOLLO.
>   A beauteous soul—be that inside;
>   But outward wear so gross a hide

That on you one can scarcely look.
Let your heart contain a book
Of every kind of precious tale,
Yet not one heard—your tongue shall fail.
And now I think my task is done;
So father, freely greet your son.

> (APOLLO *floats back up amid the branches as the*
> FATHER, MOTHER, *and* MIDWIFE *come to life*
> *again. The* FATHER *unwraps the swaddling from*
> *the baby's face. Pause. The* FATHER *weeps quietly*
> *for a moment, then calms himself. He replaces the*
> *swaddling over the baby's face.)*

FATHER. Oh, wasted words.

MOTHER. Husband!

MIDWIFE *(to the* MOTHER*)*. Hush.

FATHER. Oh, wasted dreams.

MOTHER. Husband!

MIDWIFE. Hush.

FATHER *(to the baby)*. I'd ask you to forgive me—but you
    were not born, not even conceived. *(Rising to his feet)* Visit
    my dreams no longer, you who never were. I'll dream of a
    son. Someday, a son.

MOTHER. Husband!

MIDWIFE. Hush, I said.

FATHER. No more idleness. Back to my shoes.

(*The* FATHER *exits.*)

MOTHER (*calling after the* FATHER). You promised! If it were a boy, you promised!

MIDWIFE. Be quiet. The thing is done.

MOTHER (*to the* MIDWIFE). You said he was perfect. You said there was nothing to fear.

MIDWIFE. I spoke like a fool. Stay where you are.

> (*The* MIDWIFE *goes to the bundled baby. She picks it up and unwraps the swaddling from its face, then gazes upon it in horror.*)

MIDWIFE. Gods upon gods!

MOTHER. What is it?

MIDWIFE. A day of miracles still—yet some miracles are terrible.

MOTHER. What happened?

MIDWIFE. Nothing.

MOTHER. Tell me!

MIDWIFE. You have no son.

MOTHER. What are you holding?

MIDWIFE. You knew what might happen. You know what must be.

MOTHER *(trying weakly to rise)*. Let me look.

MIDWIFE. Stay! I told you!

MOTHER *(holding out her arms)*. Bring him.

> *(Pause)*

MOTHER *(as before)*. Give him to me.

> *(Pause)*

MOTHER *(as before)*. Do it.

> *(The* MIDWIFE *places the bundle in the* MOTHER's *hands. A silence falls as the* MOTHER *stares at the baby.)*

MIDWIFE. You are weak.

> *(Pause)*

MIDWIFE. You've been ill.

> *(Pause)*

MIDWIFE. You had a fever. You were raving. Crazy words. You imagined things. You thought you were giving birth. Your husband called me to help. Your fever is gone. You're better now, but you're weak.

> *(Further silence as the* MOTHER *stares at the baby;*

at last, she holds the bundle toward the MIDWIFE.*)*

MOTHER. These rags—they're old and filthy and tattered. What use are they? What are they doing in the house? Get rid of them.

> *(The* MIDWIFE *takes the bundle and begins to go, then turns to look back at the* MOTHER, *who is staring ahead with rapt fascination; pause.)*

MIDWIFE. What are you looking at?

MOTHER. That man.

MIDWIFE. What man?

MOTHER. Coming toward me. *(Cringing before the imagined man)* Don't pluck me, sir, I beg you. I'm still tiny and green.

MIDWIFE. You think you're a fig?

MOTHER. I'm no good to you.

MIDWIFE. Poor creature, your wits are gone.

MOTHER. Don't pluck me, please, sir!

MIDWIFE. You'll be yourself again. A little rest is all you need.

MOTHER. I'll tell you a secret, sir—a rare one, few folks know it. I'm not a fruit but a flower. Think of that. A flower, born to grow full and succulent like an apple. Sweet thought, isn't it? But I've not yet bloomed. I'm still a bud. You'll know I'm ripe when I'm golden yellow and fit neatly in your palm, soft but firm to touch. But not yet, please, sir. You won't enjoy me now at all.

MIDWIFE. A little madness is a remedy. Best let it run its course, not try to cool it like a fever. I'm no longer needed. I'll come again when I'm needed. Stay. You are weak.

> (*The* MIDWIFE *exits, carrying the bundle; the* MOTHER *continues to stare into space.*)

MOTHER. No, don't! Don't break my stem! Oh, how it hurts! You've done it! I begged you not to do it! Well, taste me now that you've got me—learn the worst of it. Oh! Your teeth are dull, your jaw is strong. You mash me at a single bite.

> (*The* MOTHER *slips from the bench onto the ground.*)

MOTHER. And now you spit me out. Such cursings you make! Bitter, am I? I warned you. It serves you right.

> (*The* MOTHER *leans her head against the bench as she speaks.*)

MOTHER. How did that rhyme go? I remember …
    Now I lay me on the ground,
    Lost and never to be found.
    Mother's limbs stretch over me,
    Too far above for cry or plea.
    What am I to her now—a pang
    Of absence where I used to hang?
    Or does some sense of me remain—
    Some sharp, sad, lingering phantom pain?

ILITHYIA. Mad god.

APOLLO. It's nothing you haven't seen before.

ILITHYIA. Not this.

MOTHER. Oh, Mother, now that I slip away from you, at last
I see you whole. You're not just any tree, but the only tree,
the tree with a name—the Lullaby Tree. And nothing that's
named can ever die. And you—you are all that creates, the
bringer of all birth, World Tree, Tree of Life. And whatever
clings to you must live. But I die, cut off from you,
unnamed. And I am happy. Can you hear me? No. I grieve
for you. Ah, Mother, you who are much greater than I but
much less wise—I wish you knew what I know now. All joy
and sorrow, laughter and tears, pleasure and hurt, desire
and fear—all, all, are masks for the eternal pain of love.
You who must suffer through each moment of eternity—
how I wish I could tell you, I am free!
  Thank you, sir, for plucking me down.
  And now—how did the rest of that rhyme go? Oh, yes
…

(She closes her eyes.)

MOTHER.
  Let foolish hope not enter me—
  Only one thought: Let be, let be.

(Silence.)

APOLLO. Dead, I think.

*(ILITHYIA floats from the tree branches down
to the ground; she touches the MOTHER on the
forehead.)*

ILITHYIA. She is gone indeed.

(APOLLO *addresses the audience.*)

APOLLO.
    Applaud, my friends, the comedy is over.
    What—silence? How could you ask enjoyment more?
    Is not this stuff from which good plays are made?
    An infant's life laid hastily to naught,
    A father dead to all but idle dreams,
    A mother slain by thunderbolts of wisdom?
    Conflict, pathos, a cheersome denouement?
    You churls! Ungrateful spectators! The worst
    I've seen as a divine Olympian showman!
    "Life is unfair," you grumble in your seats;
    I merely hold the mirror up to life.
    Besides, do you believe in me to blame me?
    You Jews and Christians, Muslims, Buddhists, Jains;
    You Taoists, Wiccans, Shintoists, Confucians;
    And you agnostics, atheists as well—
    Believers, even you who think you're not:
    Do you hold me holy, Phoebus Apollo,
    Whom none has worshipped for these thousand years,
    That you would turn your righteous blame my way?
    "Life is unfair," you say—but why tell me?
    I waste my tale on you, you senseless clods;
    For a sane world, invent some sane new gods.
    And now, you graceless creatures of a day,
    I leave the way I came—so ends our play.

(APOLLO *ascends out of sight above the stage; a
brief silence.*)

ILITHYIA. "The silence of the gods." Don't those words mean
anything anymore? *(Pause)* No, this won't do at all. *(To*

the audience) And since the highest of deities has taken to breaking the rules … so will I and talk to you. You bought your tickets, and I'm sure you're even unhappier with all this than I am. So what are we going to do about it? Well, dramaturgy's not my thing, and I can't promise you a happy ending, an unhappy one, or even an ending at all, but surely even I can do better than this botched job. With everybody's permission, I'll stage manage a little. First, a change of scene. *(Looking at the* MOTHER*)* But how to get this corpse offstage? Oh, forget verisimilitude and decorum. You're only an actress pretending to be dead. Off with you.

(*The* MOTHER *rises to her feet and exits.*)

ILITHYIA *(clapping her hands and calling offstage).*
Stagehands! Some bundled babies—five or six like the midwife took away.

(*Two informally-dressed* STAGEHANDS *enter, each with three swaddled bundles.*)

ILITHYIA *(tapping the bench).* Put them here.

(*The* STAGEHANDS *place the bundles in a row on the bench.*)

ILITHYIA. Go.

(*The* STAGEHANDS *exit;* ILITHYIA *shields her eyes with one hand and calls toward the lighting booth.*)

ILITHYIA. Lights! Can you hear me up there? I need it to be near midnight. Bring the fader down, oh, five points or so.

(The lights dim considerably; as she calls out her instructions, ILITHYIA looks back and forth between the stage and the booth.)

ILITHYIA. No, that's too much. Boost up a few instruments. A bit more moonlight.

(A wash of blue-green bathes the stage.)

ILITHYIA. Not that color. Audiences don't believe in realism. It's ugly.

(The blue-green wash goes away.)

ILITHYIA. More blue gels—Rosco 260, Brigham 41, Cinemoid 20, Bilbao 30, Hickok 24, Asterisk 17, any of those if you can give me a wash, mostly from the strips. Keep the straw- and red-gelled lekos and fresnels at these same levels. But, oh, raise dimmer four up two points, drop dimmer six down one point, and raise dimmer eight up three points.

(After a few changes, the stage is washed a midnight blue.)

ILITHYIA. Hmm. Moonlight but no moon. Can you give me a Linnebach projection?

(A huge quarter moon, so vividly real that we can see its mountains and craters, appears amid the tree branches.)

ILITHYIA. A spoon-shaped hole cut out of cardboard—that's all you've got? Well, it'll have to do. How about some gobo stars?

(The sky is suddenly filled with numerous stars and galaxies—as detailed and vivid as in a planetarium.)

ILITHYIA. Just pinpricks in foil? Never mind, we can't stop and run a full tech just now.

(The sound of crickets is heard.)

ILITHYIA. Crickets? Nice touch. Someone's sharp on sound. While you're at it, I need three newborn infants crying.

(Crying babies are heard.)

ILITHYIA *(To the audience).* And so—six swaddled bundles on a stone bench, underneath the barren branches of a tree, moonlight shining amid the branches, babies crying, crickets chirping. Where are we now? I'll tell you …

(The MIDWIFE enters, carrying the abandoned baby; she has unfolded the swaddling and is looking at his face.)

MIDWIFE *(to the baby).* Too horrible to keep, too horrible to throw away.

ILITHYIA. … or maybe not. Our midwife is chatting to herself—a smoother form of exposition. I think Aristotle wrote somewhere, "Better a soliloquizing mortal than a babbling deus ex machina." Or maybe it was Horace. Or Harold Bloom. Or me. It sounds like a good rule.

MIDWIFE *(as before).* My midwife's oath—it's no help to you. I swore to bring life into the world—not to keep it here.

(Pause)

MIDWIFE. So here we are, the Place of Exposure. Here's where I'll leave you, just like I've left more others than I can remember.

(Pause)

MIDWIFE. A batch of six tonight—you'll make seven. I wonder, tomorrow morning, will anyone come hoping to claim one of you? Some barren woman who's pretended to be with child a full nine months and now must prove it? Some wealthy man who has everything except seed in his loins to make an heir? Or some strange sick soul whose heart is goaded by compassion? Some days, people come fighting one another to pick up an exposed baby. Other days, none come at all. Odd, how different days can be. But tomorrow it won't matter. (Shivering) Not one of you will survive the night, it's so bitter cold.

ILITHYIA (unheard by the MIDWIFE). Sorry. My powers of stagecraft don't extend to controlling the weather.

(The MIDWIFE bends over the bundles, peering at them one by one.)

MIDWIFE. Three dead already. Three alive and crying. I should leave things as they are. Terrible is the temptation to be kind.

(She opens one of the bundles.)

MIDWIFE. Ah, a girl—and much too lovely for the world. A lullaby—that's what you need.

(She picks up the bundle in her free hand.)

24

MIDWIFE *(singing to the bundle)*.
    Men for their leisure
    Your body would treasure
    And pay or force you for their pleasure.
    Their lust would be
    Your drudgery;
    Let's put you far beyond their measure.
    There is no lust
    Within the dust,
    And so why not be fair and just?
    Let you decay,
    Become mere clay.
    Sleep reign, as in the end sleep must.

(One of the babies' crying voices falls silent.)

MIDWIFE *(setting the bundle back down)*. Ah, you sleep now—so much better. But what about this one?

(She opens another bundle.)

MIDWIFE. A boy—a strong and strapping fellow. Boys are rarer here. I wonder—what complaint did your father find with you? No matter. Another lullaby will do.

(She picks up the bundle in her free hand.)

MIDWIFE *(singing to the bundle)*.
    Stonecutter's hands
    Like iron bands—
    Already strong as any man's.
    Such work's enough
    To make hands rough;
    Let's make for you some different plans.
    Let not your youth

Make hands uncouth;
Keep palms and fingers ever smooth—
Yes, smooth as a bone
That flesh has flown;
Let sleep eternally you soothe.

(Another baby's voice falls silent.)

MIDWIFE *(setting the bundle back down).* Yes, sleep now—so much better. But what about this one?

(She opens another bundle.)

MIDWIFE. A girl—plain but aristocratic, less fortunate than any lovely whore. A wife and mother—the worst fate I can think of. But another lullaby ends all.

(She picks up the bundle in her free hand.)

MIDWIFE *(singing to the bundle).*
A mother, you—
That is your due:
A birthèd brood you'll love and rue.
They'll laugh and cry,
They'll live and die.
But let's deny to pain its due.
May no life bloom
Within your womb:
Leave it pristine like a tomb;
And may chaste death
End all your breath;
Let sleep forever you consume.

(Another baby's voice falls silent.)

MIDWIFE *(setting the bundle back down).* Sleep, sleep, yes, that's better. *(Turning her attention to the bundle she brought with her)* You need no lullaby. You're not crying. What *are* you doing, with those twisted eyes, those twisted lips, those strange and voiceless gasps? Pleading, perhaps? If so, for life or death? Well, death is what you'll get. And now I'll leave you.

> *(Silence; the* MIDWIFE *stands still, holding the bundle.)*

MIDWIFE *(to the bundle).* May I tell you something before I go? I'd never have chosen this as a trade. It pays so little, I'm always hungry. But what choice did I have? An 11-year-old slave girl, offered apprenticeship to a midwife—and freedom someday? I jumped at the chance.
  Too young to know—much, much too young.
  They say that the world is hard for the living. Not so—the living are hard for the world. Forgive me, Goddess Ilithyia. Forgive my blasphemy.

ILITHYIA *(unheard by the* MIDWIFE*).* Forgiveness isn't mine to grant. What you love, what you hate—that's between you and yourself.

MIDWIFE. Oh, it's cold—so cold.

ILITHYIA *(unheard by the* MIDWIFE*).* Like I said—no control over the weather.

MIDWIFE *(to the bundle).* Don't think I'll weep for you. I've done this, oh, hundreds of times. I've only wept once—and that was the first time. It was a mistake. I learn from my mistakes.

(Pause)

MIDWIFE *(to the bundle)*. You want to know the story, don't you? Yes, stories enchant you, I can feel it. I think that you've got stories of your own to tell. But that's impossible, surely. Stories, after a mere couple of hours in the world? Stories, from a tiny mute monster? The moonlight is playing tricks on me.

ILITHYIA *(unheard by the* MIDWIFE*)*. Pretty good moonlight after all.

MIDWIFE *(to the bundle)*. It was the first birth I attended. My mistress—she wouldn't let me do a thing. Understandable, I suppose. I was a child, after all. There I was, my fingernails trimmed and my hands smoothed with oil, and nothing to do. I couldn't even say a word—those were my orders.
   I was young.
   I despaired.
   My mistress's helpers—they pressed the mother's belly, counted out her breaths for her, shaped her dilation with fluent incantations and yet more fluent fingertips, and drew the baby down through the crescent-shaped hole in the birthing chair.
   They held him their hands.
   He cried without prompting, fine and valiant, such a strong little creature. And then the mistress cut his cord and wrapped a moist bit of cloth around its end. And then she dried him and sprinkled him with powdered aphronitrum.
   And finally—at long, long last!—my mistress handed the baby to me, with a handkerchief soaked in olive oil.
   "Touch his eyes," she told me. "Oh, so carefully. Just enough to brush away the dregs of the womb."

And so I did, as gingerly and tenderly and lovingly as I ever did anything my life, before or since.

And then—the familiar thing. My mistress swaddled the boy, laid him on the floor, and we waited for the father.

He came quickly—a brusque and impatient man. He didn't bother with rhyme or niceties. He opened the bundle without a word.

He seemed dismayed but not surprised.

"His eyes are wrong," he said.

Silence fell.

Then my mistress strode toward me.

She slapped me across the face.

"It's the girl's fault," she growled at the father and mother. "She pressed the eyes too hard."

The mother lowered her head.

The father glared at me, blaming me with his look.

He would not raise up the child.

And so it was my task to carry the baby here—to this Place of Exposure.

I wept the whole way—cried much harder than the baby, who knew nothing of what would become of him.

I wept from guilt—and worse than that, from pity.

His eyes—they were my fault.

The moon was quartered, like this. The night was cold, like this. Six babies rested here, like now. Three were dead already, while three lived and cried—yes, like tonight. But I knew no lullabies then.

I laid the baby down and opened the bundle for one last look at his face.

And then I realized …

The father's eyes were green.

The mother's eyes were blue.

The baby's eyes were brown.

It was another man's baby—a bastard.

My mistress—she had blamed me for fear of offending

the father, and out of contempt for my childhood and slavery.

The father had allowed the blame to be put on me.
And I had accepted the blame—such a fool.
My tears stopped.
My pity ended forever.
I knew none ever again.
My anger began.
I've been angry ever since.
But I pretend with my every breath. No one sees into my infinite meanness. No one knows that my every thought is bitter.

ILITHYIA *(unheard by the* MIDWIFE*).* Who isn't bitter? Who doesn't pretend? If everybody knew, who'd ever be lonely?

> *(Still holding the bundle, the* MIDWIFE *drops to her knees and weeps uncontrollably.)*

MIDWIFE. What's happening to me? I can't do anything. I can't do nothing. My anger's gone. I'm helpless without it, it was all I had. And now I'm filled with—something else, I don't know what. Not pity—no, not that. Help me, Ilithyia. As mean as my heart may be, I've never turned away from you, never broken my sacred oath to you—at least not in deeds. Help me, help me understand this, this—horror and joy, this loathing and longing. I'm ripping in two. It's terrible. It's splendid. *(To the bundle)* And you, you—whatever on earth are you? A devil or an angel?

ILITHYIA *(unheard by the* MIDWIFE*).* There's no difference.

> *(Footsteps are heard offstage.)*

MIDWIFE. Someone's coming. Maybe it's someone who can … No, I can't—can't face a human soul.

> *(Carrying the bundle, the* MIDWIFE *hurries toward the tree and hides among its shadows. The* STEWARD *enters and walks to the bench; as he speaks, he touches the bundles one by one.)*

STEWARD. Dead … the next one too … and the next … and the fourth … the fifth … and the sixth and last … all of them dead! Blast! There's always one left alive at this hour—or two or even three. But this night … *(Shivering)* … it's so beastly cold.

ILITHYIA *(unheard by the* MIDWIFE *or* STEWARD*).* How many times do I have to say it's not my fault?

STEWARD. And I need a live one—and right directly. Well, nothing to do except come again tomorrow—at an earlier hour, before they all fall to croaking. And may the night be warmer.

> *(As the* STEWARD *starts to walk away, the* MIDWIFE *lets out an involuntary sob. The* STEWARD *stops in his tracks.)*

STEWARD. Hold it. That's no baby—unless it's some whopping bellowing cow of a baby.

> *(Pause)*

STEWARD. Come out. Show yourself.

> *(Pause; the* MIDWIFE *struggles to stay silent.)*

STEWARD. Just my imagination, then. The night air teasing my ears.

>*(The STEWARD starts walking away again, then stops.)*

STEWARD. Do you think I'm an idiot, you there? I heard what I heard.

>*(Pause)*

STEWARD. If you don't want comfort, have it your way.

>*(The STEWARD starts walking away again; the MIDWIFE lets out another sob; the STEWARD stops and turns.)*

STEWARD. Over there somewhere, are you? Near the tree. Come on out, now.

MIDWIFE. No.

STEWARD. You want me to come to you, then?

MIDWIFE. Go away.

STEWARD *(mocking her)*. "Go away." Oh, right. The oldest trick in the book. A weeping woman in the shadows, feigning distress, a gang of thieves gathered 'round about her, ready to ambush some helpful poor bugger who happens along. I ought to go scurrying off as fast as these hairy legs will carry me.

MIDWIFE. Do it, then.

(*Pause*)

STEWARD. Look here—let's handle this like a pair of
reasonable cowards. I'll take just one step toward you, and
you take just one step out of those shadows. On the count
of three. One … two … three.

> (*The* STEWARD *steps toward the* MIDWIFE; *the*
> MIDWIFE *steps out of the shadows.*)

STEWARD. Was that so hard? (*Pause*) You have a baby.
(*Pause*) Did you come here to leave it or take it?

MIDWIFE. Neither.

STEWARD. No?

MIDWIFE. We're … out for a walk.

STEWARD. Out for a walk. On this coldest of nights, in the
Place of Exposure, and the baby's not crying, but you are.
(*Pause*) Why are you crying?

MIDWIFE. I'm … not crying.

STEWARD. No? My mistake. The tears, the sobs, they misled
me. (*Pause*) Why are you crying?

MIDWIFE. It's … private.

STEWARD. Oh, no, no, don't tell me that, you mustn't, I'm
warning you for your own good, I'm the nosiest, pryingest
bastard in the world, and piquing my curiosity like that—
well, you won't be rid of me until you tell me every piquing,
piquant detail. Tell me—tell me you're crying because
everybody else does it. It's the fashion.

MIDWIFE. It's ... the fashion.

STEWARD. Well, then. *(Pause)* Why are you crying? *(Pause)* Look, it's really a damned stupid question, even I can answer it. That's your own flesh and blood you've got in your arms—

MIDWIFE. What?

STEWARD. —and you've got to leave it here, and you're—

MIDWIFE. It's not my—

STEWARD. No, don't—don't say it. Don't insult what little brains I've got. As it happens, I can make things better. Not good, but better. I need a baby. A live baby. That's what I came here for. Give it to me. I won't eat it. At least it will live.

MIDWIFE. What do you need it for?

STEWARD. I'm steward to a wealthy man. You'd know his name, but I'd best not tell you. His wife—she's pregnant. She's so fearfully ugly, it takes a leap of imagination to guess how she got that way. But then, it surely took a leap of imagination to get her that way. She's got three months to go before the little beast pops out. But the wet-nurse's baby died just today, her dugs will dry up soon, and my master and mistress, they've got to keep her full up with milk, they're desperate for it, because the mistress, well, she's too vain in her very hideousness to suckle a baby herself. That baby—is it a boy or a girl?

MIDWIFE. A boy.

STEWARD. He'll be a slave—I know you'd rather he wasn't. But think of the work—to suck a teat for a living. Why, if he's a smart chap, he'll yank out his teeth as fast as they grow and make a whole life out of it, never do anything else. What do you say?

(Silence)

STEWARD. All right, let's assume, for the sake of strategy merely, you really are out for a walk in the cold night air with your newborn son crying for no reason. You look none too rich. Can you give him a better life than I'm offering him? (Reaching into his purse) I'll pay you good money.

MIDWIFE. You'd better have a look at him first.

STEWARD. Why? What does it matter?

MIDWIFE (holding the bundle toward him). Have a look.

(The STEWARD takes the bundle and opens it.)

STEWARD. Merciful Zeus—what monster is this? Why doesn't he bewail his very hideousness?

MIDWIFE. He's mute.

STEWARD. But is he human? A stupid question. He's too ugly to be anything else. Anyway, what does it matter? A nipple's got no eyes, that's what I always say. He'll do. I'll give you three obols.

MIDWIFE. A drachma.

STEWARD. Four obols.

MIDWIFE. A drachma.

STEWARD. Five obols.

MIDWIFE. Done.

(The STEWARD *gives her the money.)*

STEWARD. I wish I could say it was a pleasure doing business
with you. An experience to remember, anyway.

(The STEWARD *starts to walk away again.)*

MIDWIFE. Stop. Wait.

(The STEWARD *stops and turns toward her.)*

MIDWIFE. I can't take your money.

STEWARD. Why not?

MIDWIFE. It's not my baby. I was the midwife. The father—
he wouldn't raise him.

STEWARD. Honesty rears its ugly head.

MIDWIFE. I tried to tell you.

STEWARD. So it fell to you to get rid of him. I don't envy you.

MIDWIFE. It's nothing. It's easy. I do it all the time.

STEWARD. Oh. *(Pause)* Why are you crying?

MIDWIFE. I don't know.

STEWARD. Honesty and more honesty. Soon we'll choke on it.

MIDWIFE (*holding out the coins*). Here.

> (*The* STEWARD *takes the coins and puts them in his purse.*)

STEWARD. Goodbye, then, mysterious weeper over monsters. May all the births you attend from this time forth end in happy Raisings.

> (*The* MIDWIFE *laughs through her tears.*)

STEWARD. Is something funny?

MIDWIFE.
> Let foolish hope not enter me—
> Only one thought: Let be, let be.

STEWARD. A good rhyme, and a wise one. I'll remember it.

> (*The* STEWARD *exits.*)

ILITHYIA (*to the* MIDWIFE, *who still can't hear her*). A good clean exit. You should do the same.

> (*The* MIDWIFE *turns toward the six bundles and stares silently at them for a moment.*)

ILITHYIA (*as before*). What are you thinking, woman? Of taking a dead one home? They're not yours to worry over. The dustman will cart them away tomorrow morning. Go.

> (*The* MIDWIFE *exits.*)

ILITHYIA. *(to the audience)* I've done it—against my better judgment. Who can say what I've set in motion? The play's not over, not by any means. The baby lives, and the story takes on a life of its own. I'm not needed. And I'm happy not to know what comes of it. But you—well, you bought your tickets, and you mustn't go home yet. Don't let the management cheat you. This act is over, so get up and stretch your legs and use the facilities. I don't know if they serve drinks in the lobby, but if they do, drink as much as you can get down in ten minutes or so, you'll undoubtedly need it. *(Pause)* But—just how am I supposed to make my own exit? Mustn't be too abrupt. A last little flurry of eloquence to cap things off. Oh, I think I've got it. A benediction, a malediction; a blessing, a curse—call it what you will.

> *(She looks off in the direction where the STEWARD exited with the baby.)*

ILITHYIA.
> Grow up, grow up, unsightly whelp;
> Grow up with someone else's help.
> A monster may you always be,
> Yet filled with strange divinity.
> Become this prodigy I urge:
> To fools and wise alike a scourge.
> Strip off all folly and facades
> From human souls and also gods.
> That's enough—and just in time,
> For I'm completely out of rhyme.
> Farewell!

> *(She rises from the ground and ascends out of sight above the stage; the lights fade as the first act ends.)*

ACT II

(An early afternoon. The tree stands upstage center, mostly barren as before. The bench has been moved stage right. Stage left is a hole with a mound of earth beside it. The STEWARD enters, followed by AESOP, who is carrying a shovel. Together they walk to the hole.)

STEWARD. Now mark me close, mute ugly devil, and heed my orders—though they're the same orders I've given you daily since you grew big enough to hold a spade.

This hole you began digging yesterday—dig it deeper today.

"Why dig deeper?" ask you.

"So you may be of use," answer I.

"Why must I be of use?" ask you.

Impertinent question!

"So you may eat," answer I.

"Why must I eat?" ask you.

You wax interrogatory, and yet I'll indulge you.

"So you may live," answer I.

"Why must I live?" ask you.

Ah, you think you've got me stumped with *that* one. Your life has been of no evident value since your horrid jaws first sprouted teeth, and you became useless to keep the wet-nurse's dugs all moist and plump, and you grew into a brute capable of nothing but digging holes. And yet I have an answer.

"So *I* may have something to live for," say I. "To be a steward over slaves like you. And a steward's work is to give orders. And a live slave is more prone to obey orders than a dead one."

"And more prone to disobey, as well," say you.

"Which is what my cudgel is for," say I. "And my

prowess with it is one more justification for my life. And I like living." And there ends our learned discourse. Why do you always challenge me to these debates, when you know you're bound to lose?

So start digging.

(AESOP *starts digging.*)

STEWARD. Now that I've got you working at something properly pointless, I must peremptorily depart, for the master has summoned me on some urgent matter.

"What matter might that be?" ask you, as you always do.

"I don't know," answer I, as I always do. "But you can be sure he's got his privates tied up in a most inextricable knot over something trivial, and whatever he says will drag me away from whatever scant meaningful work I've got."

Now the master—as I've told you often, but am well-pleased that can't repeat—is an idiot. He's not got the intelligence of a mushroom—for verily, a mushroom manages its affairs much better than he does. Yea, the same may be said for even a stone. For what brains he has are mere stew, with all of a stew's inchoateness, and lacking even the nutritional qualities thereof. Without me to look after him, he'd be as dead as a stone in a fortnight—and all the smarter for it.

But doubtless, he will ask me for a full account of what his slaves are doing. And I will tell him all—or almost all, hoping as I always do that he'll forget about you.

And as he always does, he'll remember you. You are the ugliest slave on the entire island of Samos, so not even a mushroom or a stone could forget you.

"What is the ugly mute one doing?" he will ask, as he always does.

And I will tell him, as I always do, "I've got him digging holes."

And he will ask, as always does, "Why is he digging holes?"

And I will reply, as as I always do, "So he may fill them later."

"Oh," he will say, fully satisfied, for by then his scrotum will have drawn his attention toward more carnal matters. For well you know—although I am grateful that you can never speak it—the master likes to fornicate with sheep because his wife is too ugly and his daughters too old. And he will yearn to hie his ornery groin to yon meadow.

But—hold it now.

(AESOP *stops digging.*)

STEWARD. Take note of this tree—*Ficus carica,* the common fig, though of most uncommon stature. Observe the breadth of its trunk, the robustness of its limbs. Odd, I've never stopped to look at it before. A reverend specimen. Though dormant for the winter, it's clearly alive—observe its scattering of leaves. Be careful of its roots as you dig. Don't want to do it harm.

(AESOP *starts digging again. The* STEWARD *moves toward the tree.*)

STEWARD. Hold it now.

(AESOP *stops digging. The* STEWARD *stares at the tree in silence for a moment.*)

STEWARD. I happen to know a story about a tree such as this. There once was a prophet. A prophet of love. Went around preaching that there was nothing but love. Even the gods were nothing but love. In fact, there were no gods, since love was the only real thing there was. Inhuman teaching it was, just awful, terrifying to think about.

Well, naturally, the authorities put a death sentence upon the wretch for saying such a thing. He right well knew they would all along—knew they had no choice, what else could they do? He went to the big city to turn himself in.

On his way there, along the road, he and his followers came across a fig tree—like this one. And like now, it wasn't the season for figs, too early for them. A perfectly healthy fig tree with a few leaves on it, but no figs. The prophet was hungry, and on his way to his own execution—but no figs.

He got angry. He said to the tree, "Let no man eat your fruit, from this time forever." And the tree withered at once, and all its leaves fell.

And the prophet's followers stared on with horror. They murmured to each other, "How quickly the fig tree withered away!"

And the prophet overheard them and said, "Love with all belief, believe in nothing but love. For whoever loves completely, with all his heart, may say to a mountain, 'Go away from this place and throw yourself into the sea,' and that very thing will happen. If you love completely, with all your heart, whatever you command will come to pass."

Odd sort of story.

A prophet of love, but so full of rage that he murdered a tree.

Can't get my head around it, somehow.

(The STEWARD *and* AESOP *stare at the tree for a moment.)*

STEWARD. But you know, I almost half believe it. The whole world, the whole universe—nothing but love everywhere, as far as the eye can see, as far as the ear can hear, as far as thought can reach. Gnaws at my guts to consider it, but it seems true somehow. Wish it weren't, but there's no way around the truth, once it gets stuck inside you.

Which is why I'd never tell this story to anyone but a mute idiot like you.

There'd be real hell to pay if such a truth got out.

Think of what would happen.

No one would take thought for anything in life—not what they ate, nor what they drank, nor what clothes they wore. For behold the birds of the air: they don't sow, nor do they reap, nor do they gather into barns, yet they stay well-fed. And consider the lilies of the field: they don't work, nor do they spin, and yet they go more handsomely clothed than the richest princes of the earth.

But we're not birds, and we're not lilies.

How could we bear such a life?

Happier digging holes, we are.

(Silence)

STEWARD. But why are you goading me on to yammer such nonsense, lazy beast? Start digging. I'll go report to the master that I've got everybody properly working.

> *(The STEWARD exits. AESOP digs alone for a moment. Then the PRIESTESS enters.)*

PRIESTESS. Pardon me, good fellow. I do hope you can help me.

> *(AESOP looks up from his digging, turns, and sees her. He waves jauntily, turns away, and resumes digging. Then—a perfect double-take—he looks at her again. Stricken with awe, he drops his shovel, rushes to her, and prostrates himself at her feet.)*

PRIESTESS. What's this?

> *(On his knees, AESOP extravagantly waves his arms and salutes her with bows, salaams, and genuflections.)*

PRIESTESS. Oh, my ceremonial garb! No, friend, I'm not a goddess. Just a priestess of Isis.

> *(AESOP rises. With an annoyed, dismissive gesture, he stomps away, picks up his shovel, and resumes digging, facing away from her.)*

PRIESTESS. I tried to find a shortcut to the city, and now I'm lost—and tired, and aching, and hungry, too. Can you tell me the way back to the highway?

> *(AESOP stops digging, shakes his head vigorously at her, then turns away and digs again.)*

PRIESTESS. Churl! Surely you know.

> *(Again AESOP stops digging, turns toward her, reaches inside his mouth, pulls out his tongue by its tip with his fingers, and lets go of it. It falls limply to his chin. He takes hold of it with his fingers again, rolls it up, and stuffs it back inside his mouth.)*

PRIESTESS. Oh. You are mute.

> *(With an affirmative snap of his fingers, AESOP nods, turns away, and digs again. The PRIESTESS sits on the bench and speaks to the audience. AESOP stops digging during her speech, sets his shovel aside, and listens intently.)*

PRIESTESS. Well. I may speak frankly, I suppose. I'm sure
    you won't tell my tale—and this poor drudge couldn't if
    he wanted to. I left Egypt years ago to spread worship of
    the goddess Isis throughout the world, and to heal in her
    name. Through Ethiopia and Mesopotamia and Ionia
    I've traveled, and on this isle I begin my journey through
    Greek lands. Oh, the multitudes I've touched! The wounds
    and ailments I've tended! Fractures and fevers, retching
    and rheumatism, sadness and sores! Madness, dementia,
    demonic possession! Colds and consumption, coughing
    and cholera! Swollen red bites of spiders, vipers, dogs
    gone mad! Festering blisters and boils that oozed and
    stank to the skies! Amid regions of plague, epidemic, and
    pestilence I've wandered. Over each ailing soul I met,
    I waved reeking censers of incense, sang prayers and
    incantations till my throat grew raw, applied poultices
    and plantain leaves, spread balms and aloes, served teas
    and broths. Some folks got better, some got worse. Some
    lived, some died. What *I* did never mattered. Never in all
    my travels did I heal a soul, much less raise from the dead.
    Not one single miracle—no evidence of Isis, ever. "Surely,"
    I thought, "someone will see through this sham. Surely I'll
    be crucified, burned, or flayed alive for the charlatan I am."
    But here I sit before you alive. Did anyone doubt me? No.
    One poor woman in Palestine, with an issue of blood she'd
    suffered twelve long years, crept behind me as I walked.
    "No need to trouble the priestess," I heard her murmur
    beneath her breath. "I'll touch the hem of her gown, and I'll
    be whole." No virtue passed from me with that touch, and
    she bled as badly as before. But she was ecstatic. "It is the
    will of Isis that I bleed!" she cried. "Isis be praised!" That
    was always the refrain, everywhere I went, from everyone
    I touched, in wellness and life, in sickness and death. "It is
    the will of Isis! Isis be praised!" I alone ceased to believe.
    There is no Isis. And yet—what does my life mean if not to
    serve her?

>   (AESOP *lets out a sharp whistle. The* PRIESTESS *looks at him.*)

PRIESTESS. Well? What do you want?

>   (*Patting his stomach and pointing to his mouth,* AESOP *pantomimes that he is hungry.*)

PRIESTESS. So what? I'm hungry too.

>   (AESOP *makes signs for the* PRIESTESS *to give him something to eat.*)

PRIESTESS. If I had something to eat, I'd gladly share it.

>   (AESOP *points to her, then lies down on the ground.*)

PRIESTESS. No—I *don't* lie!

>   (AESOP *leaps to his feet and walks to the fig tree. He points and gestures to it excitedly.*)

PRIESTESS. A fig tree.

>   (AESOP *pantomimes picking figs off the tree and eating them.*)

PRIESTESS. No figs. They're out of season.

>   (AESOP *points to the* PRIESTESS, *then pantomimes working a magical spell on the tree.*)

PRIESTESS. Are you deaf as well as dumb? I just said I have no powers.

(AESOP *continues his pantomime.*)

PRIESTESS *(rising to her feet and walking toward the tree).* I'll prove it, then.

(*The* PRIESTESS *chants and moves about the tree.*)

PRIESTESS.
  Blither blather,
  Do that voodoo
   People think I do so well.
  Pretty soon
  You'll see I'm phony,
   And you'll tell me, "Go to hell!"

(*The* PRIESTESS *steps away from the tree and brushes her hands together.*)

PRIESTESS. There. What do you think of my powers now?

(AESOP *jumps up and down and points excitedly at the tree—for indeed, a single fig has appeared there. He plucks it from the tree and shows it to the* PRIESTESS.)

PRIESTESS. What's this? A ripe, juicy fig! *(To the fig)* Where did you come from, little fellow? You must have been there all along. I didn't notice you.

(AESOP *makes a gallant display of offering the fig to the* PRIESTESS.)

PRIESTESS. Oh, no. You found it. Go on and eat it.

(*With elaborate courtesy,* AESOP *continues to offer her the fig.*)

PRIESTESS. I insist.

(AESOP *drops to his knees and implores her with flamboyant signs to accept the fig.*)

PRIESTESS. I'm not worthy.

(AESOP *rises to his feet and brusquely—even rudely—shoves the fig into her hands. He steps away from her and crosses his arms.*)

PRIESTESS. Well—thank you. May we share it?

(AESOP *shakes his head curtly.*)

PRIESTESS. If you insist.

(*The* PRIESTESS *sits back down on the bench and starts eating the fig.* AESOP *steps toward the tree, and imitating the* PRIESTESS's *manner, silently mouths a prayer for more figs.*)

PRIESTESS. It won't work. I'm sorry.

(AESOP *gestures for the* PRIESTESS *to work her magic again.*)

PRIESTESS. I had nothing to do with it.

(AESOP *continues his pantomime.*)

PRIESTESS. I can't. I've more than proved it everywhere. Isis isn't with me. I don't believe Isis is anywhere.

(AESOP's *pantomime becomes more frenetic.*)

PRIESTESS. Must you rub my nose in my powerlessness?
Cruel slave!

(AESOP *continues his pantomime.*)

PRIESTESS. Promise me this will be the last time.

(AESOP *assures her with vigorous nods and
gestures. The* PRIESTESS *approaches the tree and
halfheartedly prays as before.*)

PRIESTESS.
Goddess Isis,
You for whom
I've ceased possessing all belief,
I call on you
Now to defy me:
Bring forth a bit of fruit and leaf.

(*Scattered leaves and clusters of figs sprout on the
tree.* AESOP *breaks into a joyous dance.*)

PRIESTESS. I don't believe it.

(AESOP *shrugs flippantly, then continues dancing.*)

PRIESTESS. I must be dreaming.

(AESOP *pinches her sharply on the backside.*)

PRIESTESS. Ow!

(AESOP *dances some more.*)

PRIESTESS. How dare you!

(AESOP *stops dancing and pinches his own backside. He throws back his head and opens his mouth in a silent cry of pain. Then he points to her, enjoining her to do the same.*)

PRIESTESS. Pinch *myself* to prove I'm awake?

(AESOP *nods enthusiastically.*)

PRIESTESS. Oh, this is silly, but—

(She pinches herself on the arm.)

PRIESTESS. Ow! I *am* awake!

(AESOP *points to the priestess, then again pantomimes working a magical spell on the tree.*)

PRIESTESS. No. You promised—only that once.

(AESOP *continues his pantomime.*)

PRIESTESS. I'm not some cheap conjuror. I'm not here to do tricks for your entertainment.

(Again, AESOP *rubs his belly and points to his mouth.)*

PRIESTESS. And not for your nutrition, either.

(AESOP *makes an angry gesture, hunches his shoulders, stomps back to his shovel, and resumes digging. The* PRIESTESS *stares at the tree.*)

PRIESTESS. And yet—oh, sweet Isis, what am I to make of this?

(She chants and moves about the tree, more earnestly than before.)

PRIESTESS.
>Blessèd goddess,
>Sovereign spirit,
>>In whom all is manifest,
>Forgive your servant
>Her presumption,
>>Putting your name to the test.
>Mother Isis!
>All that's holy!
>>Let this lowly tree be blessed!

(With a hearty rustling sound, the tree erupts with leaves and figs. AESOP glances over his shoulder at this transformation, shrugs indifferently, and keeps digging. The PRIESTESS stares at the tree silently for a long moment, then speaks.)

PRIESTESS. A little boy in Tarsus lay dying in his bed of straw. A tumor in his belly swelled up huge and fat—like the moon when she looms so full and near, mortals fear she'll crash into the earth. I watched as tears rolled from the ruins of his eyes—salty tears mingled with salty blood. I listened as his lungs rumbled and heaved like a blacksmith's bellows. But through his pain, he refused to cry out, or even to let forth the smallest moan.

As I began my prayers for him, he murmured …

"O Priestess, do not cure me. Beg Isis for the gift of death."

"But child," I replied, "if you live, I promise you a perfect life—in Isis's name, I promise it! You'll live long and long, blessing with joy and lovingkindness your mother and father, your brothers and sisters and friends—

and someday a wife and children and grandchildren. Your companions will adore you, the world will honor you, for you'll be a laughing hero to all, doing good works wherever you go. I promise, you'll live without another moment's twinge of pain or sorrow. No hurt, no sickness, no lost loved ones, no disappointments or humiliations. And when you must die, scores of years from now, it will be in your bed, without word or worry, vanishing forever into the warm embrace of some sweet dream!"

Then he told me …

"Somewhere in this world, someone else feels hurt like mine. If I get well, others will sicken and hurt. If I never hurt again, the world will still be full of hurt. I won't live in a world that has hurt in it. Tell Isis to let me die."

I prayed his prayer to you, O Goddess.

You did nothing.

My hand is long and wide. I placed it on his face. It covered his brow, his nose, his lips, his chin. I pressed with all my weight.

His body heaved. His soul longed for death, but his flesh cleaved to life. Yet he was weak. His struggle lasted only a moment. Then he was gone. I offered you no prayer of thanks, O Goddess. It was not your doing—not your mercy.

But now you give me cause to pray again.

(AESOP *has stopped digging and is listening to her. The* PRIESTESS *raises her hands to the sky.*)

PRIESTESS.
O living nature, mother universal;
Initial progeny of worlds and worlds,
Primordial child of matter, time, and space,
And governess of energies divine;
O queen of heaven, principal of gods,

Celestial light of all the goddesses;
You by whose will the planets of the air,
The wholesome salty breezes of the seas,
The silences of darkest hell itself
Are all disposed: you, you are what you are,
Without whom nothing else may ever be—
For truly, you're the only thing that is.
Water and fire and air, and yea, the earth—
All, all is Isis, Isis, naught but you.

(*The* PRIESTESS *examines the fig she has started eating.*)

PRIESTESS. Far and wide, I've prayed to you for bliss in life or release in death. I've scarce met a mortal anywhere who didn't beg me for one or the other. I've prayed and prayed and prayed for all your children everywhere, in their vast implacable wretchedness. And how do you answer me at long, long last? With a fig!

(*She crushes the fig in her fist.*)

PRIESTESS.
Happy I am, now that you've shown yourself,
Flaunting your nature through this vicious joke,
So I, once-doubting sycophant of yours,
May know you and believe in you and hate you—
Yes, hate you, and all the rotting seepage
Gushing alive from your infected womb.
For what are you but some incestuous whore
Obscenely fornicating with yourself
Atop unbounded wastes of excrement,
The dungheap of your own created chaos?
What are you, truly, but a scabby cur,
A worm-infested, rancid bitch in heat,

Within whose guts all life is foul disease,
And I—I nothing but a poxied sore?

(She throws the fig away.)

PRIESTESS. As long as you were silent, I was powerless.
So thank you, thank you, goddess, for this sign. Now I
know my mission—to retrace my steps, undo the faith
I've engendered, and slay every living thing I meet, from
the loathèd housefly to the belovèd child at play, till not
so much as a blade of grass remains alive in all creation.
Since all that lives is part of you, I'll murder you piecemeal,
ending with myself. I'll begin my sacred work right here.

*(She turns toward the tree and raises her hands
toward it; AESOP watches.)*

PRIESTESS.
Ugly canker,
Filthy lesion,
Stinking with the filth of life,
However dare you
Add your anguish
To a world that weeps with strife?
From all that lives,
Gross and repugnant,
I'll cut you with my tongue, my knife.

*(The tree, with massive aching groan, twists and
shrivels until it stands dead, barren, and silent. The
stage is darkened. Both the PRIESTESS and AESOP
stare at the tree for a long moment. At last, the
PRIESTESS gently touches its trunk.)*

PRIESTESS. Poor tree. Was it your fault that you were part
of Isis's body? No, for you never shared her evil will. You

didn't deserve my rage. And yet—if I can—if I could—should I give you life again? You're at peace now. Never again will you fear the woodman's ax, the lightning's blast, the cold wind blighting leaf and flower, men stealing your fruit—your precious unborn children. It's over now—your mute endurance of the goddess's cruelty. I acted out of rage, but I worked a deed of mercy. And now, from pity and nothing else, I'll cut a swath of death throughout the globe, peeling it of life like an apple of its skin.

> (*Another pause. The* PRIESTESS *catches* AESOP's *eyes again; he looks away from her and anxiously resumes his digging.*)

PRIESTESS. Pardon me, good fellow.

> (AESOP *stops digging and stares at her apprehensively.*)

PRIESTESS. Can you show me the way back to the highway?

> (AESOP *continues staring at her.*)

PRIESTESS. Or the shortest way to the city?

> (*They gaze at each other in silence; then* AESOP *resumes digging.*)

PRIESTESS. Don't be unkind to a lost and hungry stranger. Just point the way.

> (AESOP *digs.*)

PRIESTESS. I'll not conceal my purpose. You know it already.

> (AESOP *digs.*)

PRIESTESS. You share my wish to end all life. You, a poor mute slave who has never tasted a moment's joy—how could you not?

(AESOP *digs.*)

PRIESTESS. I have the power. You have none. So help me. Point the way.

(AESOP *digs.*)

PRIESTESS. Point the way! I command you!

(AESOP *stops digging and stares at her.*)

PRIESTESS. No. I'll not command. I'll not be angry. Just—just—please, show me the way. Then I'll put a good end to you.

(Pause)

PRIESTESS. I understand. You're like the boy. Your soul longs for death, but your flesh cleaves to life. I'll ask nothing more of you.

(She raises her hands to AESOP, who continues staring at her.)

PRIESTESS.
    Lowly creature,
    Most unhappy,
        For mercy alone I now do this.
    Shall it pain you
    Just an instant,
        Or rather feel like a lover's kiss?

Let your death
Be sweet and simple,
    Your life's one moment of true bliss.

*(Thunder and lightning. The trunk of the tree
opens like a massive double door, and out of it
steps* MNEMOSYNE, *the very image of divine
radiance. The* PRIESTESS *throws her hands over
her eyes, almost blinded;* AESOP *seems unfazed
and unsurprised. Thunder and lightning continue as*
MNEMOSYNE *speaks.)*

MNEMOSYNE.
    Your incantation I now quell,
    Annulling its life-hating spell.
    This fellow's breast shelters a spark
    That shimmers in the fearful dark—
        A spark of untold glory,
        A spark of sacred story.
    At my implacable command,
    Let that feeble spark be fanned,
    Then fed with fuel—coal and peat—
    Until it blazes white with heat.
        Let the poor man live;
        Let him his story give.

*(The thunder and lightning stop. The stage is
brilliantly lit with an unearthly, golden glow. The*
PRIESTESS *slowly lowers her hands from her face,
squinting from the goddess's brilliance.* AESOP
*watches on with an inscrutable expression. As she
speaks, the* PRIESTESS *grows accustomed to the
light, and her eyes widen wildly.)*

PRIESTESS. But lo! The goddess herself deigns—or should I
    say dares?—to appear, thwarting my act of charity. So *this*

is the manifestation that you choose, from your hundreds of thousands of divine and multicolored forms! Oh, you are dazzling, certainly—clothed in celestial garlands and garments, your body smeared with suffocating sweet perfumes, your face a scorching effulgence. Surely I'm meant to be dashed, destroyed, vaporized by your stunning mystic opulence. Alas, no. The hosts of demons and sages may flee you, and all the planets with their demigods may be disturbed and quail at the sight of you—but not I. Come, don't hold back. Appear instead in your infinite universal form, adorned with uncountable crowns and weapons, with numberless faces, eyes, arms, thighs, legs, bellies, and gaping mouths filled with terrible teeth, your entire divinity extending everywhere, without beginning, middle, or end, spreading throughout the stars and all spaces among them, blazing like hundreds of thousands of suns rising at once into the sky. Smite me in your fullest and most terrible manifestation—I dare you to try it. Though I be but little, I am fierce. My hatred for you has made me your peer.

(Pause)

MNEMOSYNE. Who *are* you?

PRIESTESS. You know.

MNEMOSYNE. I think not.

PRIESTESS. I am your priestess.

MNEMOSYNE. I know all my priestesses. I don't remember you. And you have a most peculiar way of showing your devotion.

PRIESTESS. Here's my devotion!

> (*The* PRIESTESS *takes her sacred stole off her shoulders, spits on it, and throws it to the ground.*)

MNEMOSYNE (*picking up the stole*). Thank you, it's quite lovely—although the spitting seems an odd sort of ritual, certainly not what I'm used to from my minions. Such pretty embroidered patterns! What are they, pictograms?

PRIESTESS. They are your own sayings.

MNEMOSYNE. Oh, no, surely not. I'm not much for shibboleths and such. Besides, I don't recognize the language. (*Handing back the stole*) I'm grateful, truly, but I can't accept it. It wouldn't be proper. Routine sacrifices are the rule.

> (*The* PRIESTESS *again spits on the stole and throws it to the ground;* MNEMOSYNE *does not pick it up.*)

MNEMOSYNE. What an odd creature you are! I'm trying my best to be polite—but look at you! And what's all this nonsense about getting dashed, destroyed, vaporized, and smote? Demons, sages, and demigods, indeed! I'm not all *that* effulgent. The slave survived the sight of me, why shouldn't you?

> (*The* PRIESTESS *looks at* AESOP *with surprise.* AESOP *shrugs. The* PRIESTESS *turns toward* MNEMOSYNE *again.*)

PRIESTESS. But you are the goddess.

MNEMOSYNE. *A* goddess, anyway.

PRIESTESS. There's only one.

MNEMOSYNE. One? Oh, right—there's good bit of that only-one-god-or-goddess sort of talk going around. Quite the fashion. Still, I wouldn't go saying that to just anybody—especially none of the hordes of largely redundant deities of one stamp or another. Not all of them are as easygoing as I am. Besides, you seem to have mistaken me for someone else.

PRIESTESS. The goddess Isis. I've made no mistake.

MNEMOSYNE. I've never heard of any Isis.

PRIESTESS. Liar.

MNEMOSYNE. Oh, really, this is too much. I've got half a notion to smite you after all. I *have* done my share of smiting in my day. But no, I don't think so. I learned long ago that it's no real pleasure in life. Besides, my business here isn't with you. It's with that fellow there.

PRIESTESS. The slave?

MNEMOSYNE. Destiny is no respecter of persons. He has a mighty purpose to fulfill. I sensed it—a story in the making. I don't yet know what sort of story, but it will be sweeping, magnificent, cataclysmic—apocalyptic, even. That's why I came—to stop you from snuffing it out before it got started, you vulgar philistine.

PRIESTESS. Not Philistine. Egyptian, and you know it.

MNEMOSYNE. You *are* obtuse, aren't you? Well, kindly make yourself scarce. You're a nuisance, and I've got work to do.

PRIESTESS. I'll not let you near him.

MNEMOSYNE. And why not?

PRIESTESS. He's mine to destroy—just as I did this tree.

MNEMOSYNE. Murdered it, did you? I suppose you feel proud of yourself. But don't make too much of it. I'm pretty sure your powers of destruction are solely courtesy of his imagination—a quality you clearly lack.

PRIESTESS. My powers come from my hatred for you.

MNEMOSYNE. Oh, that's right, you've got some idea that I'm that goddess you both serve and hate. I'm not her. I am Mnemosyne.

PRIESTESS. There's no such goddess.

MNEMOSYNE. Well, technically, I'm a titaness and not a proper Olympian goddess, so you might not have heard of me. Still, go easy on the sacrilege. My patience isn't infinite; nothing is. I'm known by many epithets: Daughter of Uranus and Gaia, Consort of Zeus, Sacred Spring of Trophonios, Lovely Sister of Lethe, Mother of the Muses, and—what's that other one? I seem to have forgotten, I am getting on in years. They call me … um … oh, yes— Goddess of Memory.

PRIESTESS. Cunning lies.

MNEMOSYNE. You no longer amuse me. You never *did* amuse me. Go at once.

PRIESTESS. I'll not move from this spot until you admit who you really are.

MNEMOSYNE. I just did.

PRIESTESS. I don't believe you. Smite me if you must.

MNEMOSYNE. I'm too old for such rubbish. Younger blood
   is needed. Excuse me while I—well, invoke.

      (MNEMOSYNE *raises her arms toward the tree,*
      which still stands open. The stage darkens again;
      more thunder and lightning as she chants.)

MNEMOSYNE.
      Daughters of mine,
      Ye Muses Nine,
   Whom I conceived in Olympian scandal
      During nine torrid
      Nights when I whorèd
   With Zeus, our lust a blazing candle:
      Come to my aid
      This wench to upbraid,
   For really, she's more than I can handle.

      (The thunder and lightning stop. The stage is
      brilliantly lit with the same unearthly, golden glow
      as before. One by one, the NINE MUSES *enter*
      *from the tree—*CLIO, URANIA, MELPOMENE,
      THALIA, TERPSICHORE, CALLIOPE, ERATO,
      POLYHYMNIA, *and* EUTERPE.)

CLIO.
   Enter the Muses …

URANIA.
              … three times three.

MELPOMENE.
>Enter you ...

THALIA.
>... and enter me.

TERPSICHORE.
>I follow her ...

CALLIOPE.
>... and then comes she.

ERATO.
>Sacred sisters ...

POLYHYMNIA.
>...enter we ...

EUTERPE.
>... And promptly, quickly ...

MUSES *(together)*.
>... all nine be!

CLIO.
>Yes, here we be ...

MELPOMENE.
>... and here we are ...

URANIA.
>... Out of this tree that stands ajar ...

POLYHYMNIA.
>... Summoned forth from near and far.

THALIA.
We ladies are a busy crew …

TERPSICHORE.
… With sundry pressing things to do …

CALLIOPE.
… So tell us, tell us, tell us true …

ERATO.
… Yes, tell us, you who gave us birth …

POLYHYMNIA.
… Why call us here, in grief or mirth …

MUSES *(together)*.
… From all four corners of the earth?

MNEMOSYNE. The earth is round. It doesn't have corners.

POLYHYMNIA. Oh, Mother!

EUTERPE. We were speaking figuratively.

MNEMOSYNE. That's always your excuse for getting your facts wrong.

THALIA. What *do* you want this time?

MNEMOSYNE *(leaning against the tree)*. I'll tell you, but give me a moment to catch my breath. I've just done two big invocations, and they take a lot out of me. I'm not the invoker I used to be. And seeing all nine of you together … it reminds me how tiring children are.

TERPSICHORE. Well, excuse *us* for disturbing your peace and quiet!

CLIO. It's not like we've got urgent business.

EUTERPE. Not at all.

CALLIOPE. Only civilization is at stake.

MELPOMENE. If we loosen our inspirational grip on these, these …

ERATO. … these inadequately-evolved so-called creative genius mortals …

THALIA. … even for so much as a teeny tiny moment …

URANIA. … cultures everywhere are liable to unravel …

POLYHYMNIA. … leaving humankind in utter and unredeemable chaos and savagery.

CLIO.
     So tell us truly, is this pressing?
     Not as much—or so I'm guessing—
     As helping out Herodotus
     A bunch of battles to discuss.
     I must stick by him, not be lax,
     For he plays fast and loose with facts.

URANIA.
     My problem's Ptolemy—prince of seers,
     His brain all full of crystal spheres.
     The very cosmos is at stake;
     Try as I might, I cannot break

His stubborn notion, fixed like granite,
The stars and sun move 'round our planet.

MELPOMENE.
A brand new breed of tragedian
Has got me feeling badly beaten.
Of simple plotting they're all scorners,
Writing their stories into corners.
Euripides wrecks sundry scenes,
Then patches them with god machines.

THALIA.
And then there's Aristophanes
Who's got me pleading on my knees
To show a wee bit of restraint.
A subtle comic—that he ain't!
He's satirized a prominent man,
And so he's getting sued again.

POLYHYMNIA.
And Pindar—that Dircaean Swan—
Has got a thing for manly brawn.
His odes start fine: he praises gods,
And all their virtues he applauds.
But in the end, he drools and gawks,
And always winds up praising jocks.

ERATO.
A sonneteer named Shakespeare's lust
Is for a lass with skin like rust
And wires sprouting from her scalp.
What's more, she's faithless—that's no help.
I must procure for him a lady
Who's not so homely or so shady.

CALLIOPE.
> James Joyce—who's Irish, I should mention—
> Is full of Homer-style pretension.
> He's got this notion, rather troublin',
> That brave Odysseus lives in Dublin.
> What's worse, in scribbling or dictation,
> He's thrown away all punctuation.

TERPSICHORE.
> In Moscow, ballet's in decline;
> The task of fixing it is mine.
> Performers lack sinew or joint
> For dancing properly en pointe.
> They're getting fat; too much they weigh
> To do a decent grand jeté.

EUTERPE.
> Then there's our playwright—no, our hack;
> When I so much as turn my back,
> He uses all his wiles and tools
> To make us characters look like fools.
> I swear, it really is a crime,
> The way we have to speak in rhyme.

CLIO. But never mind all that.

TERPSICHORE. No, think nothing of how we bear the burden of all human thought.

ERATO. Western thought, anyway.

POLYHYMNIA. Past, present, and future.

THALIA. The books and school of the ages.

URANIA. Genius with a capital G.

CALLIOPE. Tell us what you need that trumps our other
duties.

URANIA. But oh, don't put yourself out.

EUTERPE. Take your sweet time about it.

MUSES *(together)*. We're always your devoted little girls.

MNEMOSYNE *(pointing to the* PRIESTESS). It's *her*.

EUTERPE. What about her?

MNEMOSYNE *(pointing to* AESOP). She keeps getting
between me and *him*.

POLYHYMNIA. What about him?

MNEMOSYNE. I've got things to do with him.

ERATO. Oh, Mother, really!

MNEMOSYNE. Really, what?

CALLIOPE. Really—*him?*

TERPSICHORE. Are you that desperate?

THALIA. You used to have style …

MELPOMENE. … charm …

URANIA. … glamour …

CLIO. ... panache!

CALLIOPE. You were Zeus's whore!

THALIA. And he's so ... what's a polite word?

TERPSICHORE. Ugly.

THALIA. Right.

ERATO (*patting* AESOP *on the head*). I think he's cute.

OTHER MUSES (*together*). Cute?

ERATO (*stroking* AESOP's *hair*). I mean Guinea pig cute, bulldog cute, horseshoe crab cute—not Ruler-of-Olympus, King-of-Gods-and-Mortals, Wielder-of-Oak-Cleaving-Thunderbolts cute.

> (*As the dialogue continues,* ERATO *and* AESOP *sit together on the mound where he has been digging; he rests his head on her shoulder; she occasionally slaps him lightly but firmly when his hands get too free.*)

CALLIOPE. Mother, Dear Mother!

THALIA. We know you're not the beauty queen you once were, but—

MUSES (*together*). Really!

MNEMOSYNE. Be still, your dirty little minds! I don't want *that* from him. I mean to help him fulfill his destiny. (*Indicating the* PRIESTESS) But this—this *creature* keeps getting in my way.

TERPSICHORE *(to the* PRIESTESS*)*. And who are you?

PRIESTESS. I … I … I …

MUSES *(together, mockingly)*. You … you … you …

URANIA *(to the* PRIESTESS*)*. Come on, spit it out.

PRIESTESS. I am … I was …

MELPOMENE. … and doubtless ever shall be …

MUSES *(together)*. What?

PRIESTESS. A priestess of Isis.

CLIO. Isis?

EUTERPE. Who is Isis?

MNEMOSYNE. Never heard of her either, eh? Odd. She insists that Isis is the only deity there is.

URANIA. What does that make all the rest of us?

CLIO *(to the* PRIESTESS*)*. When *will* you monotheists just open your eyes and look in front of your noses?

POLYHYMNIA. Isis … The name sounds familiar.

MELPOMENE. From some archaic pantheon, no doubt.

POLYHYMNIA. I remember! Egyptian!

ERATO. Oh, yes, there's a charming little love story about her and her brother—

THALIA. Brother?

TERPSICHORE. Incest?

ERATO. Well, it *is* an Egyptian story. So sweet. He got chopped up into little pieces.

CALLIOPE. Guh-*ross!*

ERATO. It worked out happily somehow.

POLYHYMNIA (*to the* PRIESTESS). How long ago did you leave Egypt?

PRIESTESS. Many years.

POLYHYMNIA. Then you haven't heard that Isis is forgotten there.

PRIESTESS. What does it matter if she's forgotten if she exists?

POLYHYMNIA. What does it matter if she exists if she's forgotten?

EUTERPE. Existence isn't all it's cracked up to be, anyway.

CALLIOPE. Existence doesn't even exist.

THALIA. It's a sham.

URANIA. A fraud.

CLIO. A mirage.

ERATO. A trick of the light.

EUTERPE. An illusion.

MELPOMENE. All done with mirrors.

POLYHYMNIA. Wires.

TERPSICHORE. Trapdoors.

THALIA. Misdirection.

URANIA. Sleight of hand.

EUTERPE. Just a cheap conjuring stunt performed by some nonexistent mountebank.

MNEMOSYNE. So forget about your pathetic forgotten Isis. She's not real—no more than you or I or this slave or any of the rest of us.

POLYHYMNIA. And she's not worshipped. We are. That's what counts.

PRIESTESS. But—what are you going to do?

MNEMOSYNE. Fulfill the prophecy.

PRIESTESS. What prophecy?

MNEMOSYNE. That remains to be seen.

PRIESTESS. So you prophesy ... that there'll be a prophecy?

URANIA. Smart lass.

THALIA. I think she's got it.

MNEMOSYNE. Nothing of the sort. She's as stupid as a post, but infinitely more noisy. I'll never get my work done with all her meddling questions and brainless blasphemies. What am I to do with her?

ERATO *(rising to her feet).* You really *are* losing your faculties, aren't you?

TERPSICHORE. Poor dear!

POLYHYMNIA. Why, you taught us the requisite incantation ages ago.

MNEMOSYNE. Did I? It must be something quite elaborate. Even if I remembered it, I'm sure I couldn't manage it.

MELPOMENE. Allow us.

> *(The* MUSES *group together and glare forebodingly at the* PRIESTESS.)

MUSES *(together).* Sit!

> *(Stunned, the* PRIESTESS *sits on the bench and stares mutely at the others.)*

MNEMOSYNE. Oh, *that* incantation!

EUTERPE. Right.

ERATO *(resuming her seat next to* AESOP). She won't move from that spot or make a sound until you release her from the spell.

MNEMOSYNE. That might be a long time.

CLIO. You *do* remember the incantation-for-release, don't you?

CALLIOPE. We'd better remind you.

MNEMOSYNE. No, it'll come back to me or it won't.

URANIA. And now, may we get back to our sundry tasks?

(MNEMOSYNE *approaches* AESOP.)

MNEMOSYNE. Not yet. I'm feeling more addled by the moment. I arrived here in a fit of divine instinct. But now I'm at a loss. I don't know a blessed thing about this fellow—or what I'm supposed to do with him.

TERPSICHORE. Are you sure you got the right chap? He's *such* a fright to look at!

ERATO. Appearances aren't everything.

TERPSICHORE. No, indeed—they're the *only* thing.

MNEMOSYNE. It's no mistake, I'm sure.

MELPOMENE. What's his name?

MNEMOSYNE. I don't know.

THALIA. Don't know?

MNEMOSYNE. I'm not omniscient.

URANIA. Why don't you just ask him?

MNEMOSYNE. With all the chatter that's been going on?

ERATO (to AESOP). What's your name, sweetheart?

(AESOP *sits motionless and silent.*)

CALLIOPE. Not exactly talkative.

MNEMOSYNE. I don't believe he's said a word since I met him.

POLYHYMNIA. That doesn't bode well.

THALIA. It doesn't bode ill.

EUTERPE. It doesn't bode at all.

URANIA. And boding does matter.

CLIO. Boding is good.

MELPOMENE. Boding works.

THALIA. There's no such thing as bad boding.

TERPSICHORE. Oh, Mother!

CALLIOPE. You stirred up all this bodeless fuss on some half-baked hunch?

MNEMOSYNE. Not a hunch. I told you, it was *instinct.* And whatever else may be failing about me, my instinct is still sound. This humble slave has some mighty destiny to fulfill. I can feel it. And I did arrive here just in time to save his life. So I'm not *completely* incapable—not yet, anyway.

ERATO. A mighty destiny.

POLYHYMNIA. That does sound impressive.

EUTERPE. Can you give us some idea of what *sort* of destiny?

URANIA. Aside from mighty?

CLIO. Just a hint, maybe?

MNEMOSYNE. A little silence, please—so I can hear my own thoughts. *(Pause)* A story.

POLYHYMNIA. Well, yes, he *is* to be a story's hero.

CALLIOPE. Tell us something we don't already know.

MNEMOSYNE. Not the hero. More than that.

THALIA. A demigod?

MNEMOSYNE. More.

URANIA. A deity?

MNEMOSYNE. More.

ERATO. A titan?

MNEMOSYNE. More.

TERPSICHORE. Earth itself?

MNEMOSYNE. More.

CALLIOPE. Heaven?

MNEMOSYNE. More.

MELPOMENE. The mighty Alpha—that fiery void whence earth and heaven came to be?

MNEMOSYNE. More.

CLIO. The dreaded Omega—that terminal vortex into which matter, energy, time, and space must someday vanish into raptures of nothingness?

MNEMOSYNE. More.

URANIA. Well …

POLYHYMNIA. … that *does* eliminate a lot.

THALIA. It's got me stumped.

TERPSICHORE. Me too.

EUTERPE. Rath*er.*

MNEMOSYNE. He is the embodiment … the essence … the *incarnation* of story.

TERPSICHORE. But what sort of story?

MELPOMENE. Tragedy?

THALIA. Comedy?

CLIO. History?

ERATO. Pastoral?

CALLIOPE. Pastoral-comical?

POLYHYMNIA. Historical-pastoral?

MELPOMENE. Tragical-historical?

THALIA. Tragical-comical-historical-pastoral?

TERPSICHORE. Scene indivisible?

URANIA. Poem unlimited?

CALLIOPE. Oh, that, surely—an epic!

EUTERPE. Another Homer?

POLYHYMNIA. How exciting!

MNEMOSYNE. Something more than Homer.

ERATO. That word again …

CALLIOPE. … "more" …

TERPSICHORE. … it *can* be overused.

THALIA. You've certainly said it more than enough.

MNEMOSYNE. Tell me—could Homer take a lump of the blackest coal, squeeze it tightly in his fist, then open his fingers to reveal a clear, pristine diamond, ready-cut to perfection, leaving not so much as the tiniest speck of dusky powder remaining in his palm?

MELPOMENE. No.

URANIA. Who can?

MNEMOSYNE. He can.

CLIO. How wonderful!

CALLIOPE. A miraculous jeweler!

ERATO. Let's fetch a lump of coal at once!

THALIA. No, nine—a lovely diamond for each of us!

TERPSICHORE. Don't forget about Mother.

URANIA. That's right—we have her instinct to thank.

MELPOMENE. Fetch ten!

MNEMOSYNE. I was speaking figuratively.

CLIO. Oh, Mother …

EUTERPE. … we *so* wish you wouldn't do that!

POLYHYMNIA. You just don't have the metaphorical knack.

CLIO. At least not anymore. It's long gone now.

MELPOMENE. Leave such talk to younger folk.

TERPSICHORE. Whenever you try it, you just stir up confusion.

MNEMOSYNE. I should have had a tenth daughter—a Muse for fables.

ERATO. Fables?

EUTERPE. What are fables?

MNEMOSYNE. The gems this fellow can make.

URANIA. That silly metaphor again.

THALIA. And we can make sense of neither analogy nor subject …

EUTERPE. … neither vehicle nor tenor …

CLIO. … neither metaphier nor metaphrand …

CALLIOPE. … neither compar*er* nor compar*ee*.

MNEMOSYNE. No, of course you don't understand. Fables— finely storied diamonds—flourished before you were born, in the days when gods and people and animals all spoke one language.

POLYHYMNIA. Gods?

URANIA. People?

CLIO. Animals?

MNEMOSYNE. And plants. And things inert and inanimate.

MELPOMENE. Talking trees and rocks?

THALIA. The worst has happened.

TERPSICHORE. You've gone demented.

MNEMOSYNE. Don't take my word for it. Let *him* tell you.

CALLIOPE *(to* AESOP). Well?

ERATO *(to* AESOP). It's high time you said something.

POLYHYMNIA *(to* AESOP). Is our mother talking sense?

EUTERPE *(to* AESOP). Or is it time to put her away for good?

MUSES *(together)*. Tell us!

(AESOP *shrugs.*)

CALLIOPE. A shrug!

CLIO. How eloquent!

ERATO. How pithy, succinct, and succulent!

MNEMOSYNE *(approaching* AESOP). Come, good fellow.
    What have you got to say?

(AESOP *shrugs.*)

MNEMOSYNE. Nothing at all?

(AESOP *shakes his head.*)

MNEMOSYNE. I came to your aid. Now won't you come to mine?

(AESOP *shakes his head.*)

MNEMOSYNE. How can this be?

(*As he did earlier,* AESOP *reaches inside his mouth, pulls out his tongue by its tip with his fingers, and lets go of it. It falls limply to his chin. He takes hold of it with his fingers again, rolls it up, and stuffs it back inside his mouth. A startled silence falls.*)

MNEMOSYNE. He's … he's … he's …

EUTERPE. Mute.

POLYHYMNIA. Yes, that's the word.

ERATO. This embodiment …

CALLIOPE. … this essence …

TERPSICHORE. … this *incarnation* of story …

THALIA. … of gemlike fable, no less …

MELPOMENE. … cannot articulate a single solitary syllable.

MNEMOSYNE. What a ghastly mistake I've made! Unforgivable! Irreparable! Irredeemable!

URANIA. Don't take it too hard.

CLIO. You got the wrong chap, that's all.

TERPSICHORE. You merely forgot always to judge by appearances.

MELPOMENE. An honest mistake.

CLIO. An embarrassing setback.

MNEMOSYNE. Alas, daughters, it is much worse. You were quite right, senile dementia has sounded my doom, and I'm no longer competent to serve in a divine capacity. I've already made a bad job of it. Further effort will only make things worse.

URANIA. Oh, Mother, no!

POLYHYMNIA. You mustn't let this get the best of you!

EUTERPE. All will be well again.

ERATO. Some embodied essential incarnation is surely out there somewhere, desperately awaiting your aid.

CALLIOPE. You must find him …

THALIA. … and quickly!

CLIO. We'll go searching with you …

TERPSICHORE. … every last one of us!

ERATO. We'll fan out far and wide …

URANIA. … to every corner of the earth!

EUTERPE. Figuratively speaking.

MNEMOSYNE. I'll not allow it. You must get back to your singers, scribblers, fiddlers, diddlers, dabblers, hacks, and hoofers, and save what precious little there is of civilization. I've wasted too much of your time already. Please forgive me.

THALIA. But what will you do?

CALLIOPE. Where will you go?

MNEMOSYNE. Who can say? Is there a precedent for my plight—a defunct goddess? Self-slaughter is no option for immortals. I'm doomed, it seems, to infinite and eternal decay—a mysterious fate, for how can decay possibly be infinite and eternal? Mustn't there be some bottommost threshold to entropy, at which both body and soul dissipate beyond the horrors of swirling chaos into the inert heat-death of the random inane? Or shall I waste away like Echo, till there's nothing left of me but the lisping, wisping, wandering waif of my voice? I'd prefer a bang to a whimper.

> (While MNEMOSYNE *has been talking,* AESOP *has crept up behind her. He taps her on the shoulder.)*

MNEMOSYNE. Well? What do *you* want, you, you—red herring?

> (AESOP *returns to his mound, picks up his shovel, and digs again.)*

MNEMOSYNE. That's right, dig, you drudge. That's all you're good for. Oh, pardon my outburst. I *do* owe you an apology—for building up your hope, when hope is worse than useless. Thank Whatever-Powers-May-Be that most of hope remains a dreg at the bottom of Pandora's jar, where it can do nobody harm.

> (AESOP *plants his shovel in the mound, indicating with impatient gestures that* MNEMOSYNE *does not understand him. He begins to make burrowing motions with his hands and arms. His pantomime and the other characters' responses unfold like a game of charades.*)

ERATO. Oh, Mother, look what he's doing!

POLYHYMNIA. He's got a message for you!

THALIA. More than a message—a story!

CALLIOPE. In pantomime!

CLIO. He's swimming!

> (AESOP *stops burrowing, shakes his head, then starts burrowing again.*)

MELPOMENE. No, he's burrowing!

URANIA. Making like a mole!

> (AESOP *stops, nods, whistles, and points at* MELPOMENE *and* URANIA, *indicating that their responses are correct. Then he begins swinging at the ground with an imaginary pickax.*)

EUTERPE. Now he's—what?

TERPSICHORE. Mining.

CLIO. For gold.

URANIA. Silver.

POLYHYMNIA. Iron ore.

>(AESOP *stops, shakes his head, and resumes swinging again, this time gradually crouching lower and lower.*)

CALLIOPE. Oh, *I've* got it! He's not digging for anything in particular.

EUTERPE. He's digging *down,* that's all.

TERPSICHORE. Deeper and deeper into the earth.

THALIA. Way down into the bedrock.

>(AESOP *nods, resumes his burrowing pantomime for a moment, then thrashes in melodramatic pain.*)

URANIA. He's writhing from heat.

CLIO. He's gotten below the earth's crust.

ERATO. Down through the lithosphere.

CALLIOPE. Into the asthenosphere.

EUTERPE. Engulfed by molten magma.

(AESOP *nods again, then resumes burrowing with greater effort, wiping his brow from time to time because of the heat.*)

THALIA. And yet he bravely burrows deeper!

URANIA. Stout fellow!

EUTERPE. What rare yearning drives him on, I wonder?

(*As the* MUSES *continue their commentary,* AESOP *keeps on with his pantomime.*)

MELPOMENE. He's into the mantle by now.

POLYHYMNIA. The mesosphere.

TERPSICHORE. A hot and nasty place—at least the last time I was down there.

THALIA. Surely it's not improved.

URANIA. Now he's entered the outer core.

TERPSICHORE. I must say, I've never ventured that far.

CLIO. I'll bet Hades himself would find it uncomfortable.

(AESOP *stops his pickax movements, then begins the classic mime of walking in a single spot.*)

EUTERPE. And now he's …

POLYHYMNIA. … what?

ERATO. Walking against the wind?

>   (*Without stopping his movement,* AESOP *shakes his head.*)

CALLIOPE. Not wind, you silly thing.

URANIA. Not some fifty-one-hundred-and-eighty kilometers beneath the surface of the earth.

TERPSICHORE. Oh, I get it! He's reached the inner core!

URANIA. That's right—a solid crystal alloy of iron and oxygen, sulfur and nickel!

THALIA. There's no way to dig or pick or burrow through *that* hunk of metal.

MELPOMENE. He's got to walk around it.

>   (AESOP *enthusiastically nods his agreement without stopping his mime, shifting into the Michael Jackson Moonwalk, moving in a circle.*)

URANIA (*to* AESOP). Don't forget—the inner core is the hottest object in our region of the solar system.

>   (AESOP *slaps his head with self-reproach, then changes his walking mime to gingerly stepping, heel and toe, on a hot surface.*)

URANIA. There. That's more realistic.

>   (AESOP *burrows.*)

CLIO. Burrowing again.

(AESOP *pantomimes swinging a pickax.*)

POLYHYMNIA. Picking again.

(AESOP *burrows.*)

CALLIOPE. Yet more burrowing.

(AESOP *picks up his shovel and resumes digging.*)

THALIA. Yet more digging.

URANIA. We seem to have reached a kind of recapitulation.

CLIO. Only in reverse.

MELPOMENE. This narrative is getting rather circular for my taste.

EUTERPE *(to* MELPOMENE*)*. Oh, bother.

ERATO *(to* MELPOMENE*)*. *Must* all stories have a beginning, a middle, and an end?

MELPOMENE. An end, at least, is desirable.

THALIA. True.

CALLIOPE. And I, for one, see no end in sight.

CLIO. Nor do I.

(AESOP *abruptly does a handstand.*)

ERATO. Oh my goodness.

MELPOMENE. He's gone altogether upside-down.

THALIA. This *is* a mysterious sort of gesture.

TERPSICHORE. Rather nimbly done, though.

POLYHYMNIA. Symbolic, I suppose …

CALLIOPE. … of the reversal …

THALIA. … the complete inversion …

CLIO. … nay, the outright perversion …

URANIA. … of universal order.

> (AESOP *leaps to his feet, shakes his head with exasperation, then does another handstand.*)

EUTERPE. I think I understand. It's all relative.

ERATO. Right. He's not upside-down. We are.

TERPSICHORE. More precisely, there *is* no upside-down.

MELPOMENE. Nor any rightside-up.

> (AESOP *leaps to his feet, makes an encouraging gesture to indicate that the* MUSES *are getting warm, then stands on his hands again.*)

TERPSICHORE. Now I get it. It's so simple and literal, it's embarrassing.

MUSES *(together)*. Well?

TERPSICHORE. He's dug clear through to the other side of the earth.

CLIO. Then he's not standing on his head.

TERPSICHORE. He's standing on his feet.

> (AESOP *flips through the air, lands on his feet, and whistles, points, stamps, and nods with approval. He gestures during the following lines, encouraging the* MUSES' *guesses.*)

CALLIOPE. He's … he's …

CLIO. … in China.

MELPOMENE. No, India.

THALIA. No, Mongolia.

TERPSICHORE. No, Japan.

> (*After a gesture of frustration,* AESOP *begins another pantomime, somewhat similar to his burrowing.*)

CLIO. Burrowing again?

CALLIOPE. *Awfully* repetitive.

MELPOMENE. I told you, this story is entirely too circular.

> (AESOP *stops, shakes his head, and then more clearly pantomimes a swimming motion.*)

ERATO. He's swimming!

> (AESOP *whistles, points, stamps, and nods in enthusiastic approval, then resumes swimming.*)

URANIA. Of course! The diametrical opposite side of the globe from ours is nothing but a vast southern ocean!

> (*As* AESOP *alters his movements again and again, the* MUSES *correctly interpret his various mimes.*)

POLYHYMNIA. The classic crawl.

EUTERPE. The trudgeon.

URANIA. The trudgeon crawl.

THALIA. The double trudgeon.

TERPSICHORE. The double trudgeon crawl.

POLYHYMNIA. The dolphin crawl.

MELPOMENE. The breaststroke.

EUTERPE. The heads-up breaststroke.

ERATO. The butterfly.

CLIO. The slow butterfly.

CALLIOPE. The backstroke.

MELPOMENE. The inverted breaststroke.

CLIO. The inverted butterfly.

URANIA. The back double trudgeon.

EUTERPE. The immortal passado.

THALIA. The punto reverso.

MUSES *(together)*. The hay!

> (AESOP *repeats his various swimming strokes during the following commentary.*)

MELPOMENE. But what *is* he questing for?

CLIO. The Holy Grail?

THALIA. That takes a pure-of-heart sort of quester.

URANIA. He doesn't fit the profile.

TERPSICHORE. Far from it.

ERATO. The Golden Fleece, perhaps?

POLYHYMNIA. Jason nabbed it already.

EUTERPE. The subaquatic herb that grants eternal life?

CALLIOPE. Gilgamesh tracked it down, but a snake scoffed it before he could get it.

POLYHYMNIA. Maybe he's seeking a brain …

EUTERPE. … or a heart …

THALIA. … or courage …

TERPSICHORE. … or home.

CALLIOPE. Right. There's no place like home.

ERATO. You silly things, it's something more romantic. He's seeking his beloved across unspeakable vastnesses.

CLIO. Oh, like Leander for Hero.

URANIA. Well, his beloved had better be as ugly as he is—and awfully hard-up. Otherwise, he'll face sure rejection.

ERATO. Be that as it may. Leander had to swim, too.

MELPOMENE. That's right, across the Hellespont.

URANIA. But he perished, didn't he?

THALIA. And the south seas are a lot bigger than the Hellespont.

ERATO. But look—the common dog paddle.

POLYHYMNIA. The stroke of the first resort.

MUSE. That doesn't bode well.

TERPSICHORE. A sign of desperation.

TERPSICHORE. He'd better get to shore …

POLYHYMNIA. … *any* shore …

MELPOMENE. … or he's liable to drown …

EUTERPE. … or catch the ague.

> (AESOP *is really struggling now. He raises a hand with one finger pointed upward, gulps for air, holds his nose, and slips below the imaginary surface.*)

ERATO. Going down once.

> (AESOP *rises above the surface, raises a hand with two fingers pointed, gulps for air, holds his nose, and slips below again.*)

CLIO. Down twice.

> (AESOP *rises above the surface, raises a hand with three fingers pointed, gulps for air, holds his nose, and slips below again.*)

CALLIOPE. Down thrice—and that's the end of it.

EUTERPE. Somebody should save him.

POLYHYMNIA. From what? His own imagination?

> (AESOP *rises above the surface yet again; still dog-paddling, he scans the horizon in all directions.*)

ERATO. Impossible. Nobody comes up a fourth time.

CALLIOPE. It goes against time-honored shtick and lazzi.

TERPSICHORE. Nevertheless.

THALIA. Some supernatural agency must have intervened.

CLIO. A regular deus ex machina.

MELPOMENE. It wasn't us.

> (AESOP *points excitedly and breaks into a vigorous swimming stroke.*)

POLYHYMNIA. He's sighted land!

CALLIOPE. The classic crawl again.

THALIA. With more might and main than even before.

EUTERPE. A second wind like no other.

URANIA. Stout fellow!

> (AESOP *pantomimes finding land, crawling upon a beach, and kissing the sand.*)

TERPSICHORE. Terra firma at last!

MELPOMENE. A true triumph of the human spirit!

CLIO. Human spirit is a contradiction in terms.

THALIA. No need to get truthful.

ERATO. It's only a story.

> (AESOP *rises to his feet, puts his hand to his forehead, and peers all around himself.*)

CALLIOPE. He's looking for something.

CLIO. But he can't find it.

ERATO. Blinded by glaring sunlight, perhaps?

> (AESOP *stops, shakes his head, crouches with his hands on his knees, and peers some more.*)

EUTERPE. No, it's dark!

MELPOMENE. Sunless!

POLYHYMNIA. Starless!

TERPSICHORE. Moonless!

> (AESOP *enthusiastically nods his agreement, then holds his hand at various distances in front of his face.*)

THALIA. He can't see his hand in front of his face.

> (AESOP *nods again and continues peering into an imaginary darkness.*)

URANIA. The very cosmos has lost all meaning …

MELPOMENE. … gone utterly absurd.

CLIO. Talk about your basic existential angst.

TERPSICHORE. I feel a nasty spell of nausea coming on.

> (AESOP *pantomimes opening a box of matches and begins trying to strike one.*)

URANIA. Hold it right there.

EUTERPE. Matches?

POLYHYMNIA. Fresh and dry?

ERATO. After emerging from the depths of the ocean?

CALLIOPE. I hardly think so.

TERPSICHORE. Besides, matches are a bit of an
    anachronism, don't you think?

THALIA. Admittedly, this play we're in *is* crawling with
    anachronisms.

MELPOMENE. Still, this is going too far.

> *(After a shrug of reluctant agreement,* AESOP
> *embarks on a new series of pantomimes. He outlines
> a rectangular shape.)*

CALLIOPE. A board.

ERATO. A log.

THALIA. Either will do, I imagine.

> (AESOP *nods, places the object on the ground, and
> kneels beside it. He pantomimes drilling it with an
> imaginary gimlet.)*

TERPSICHORE. Boring a small hole.

> (AESOP *nods, then shapes an imaginary rod the
> length of a ruler.)*

URANIA. A stick.

MELPOMENE. But of what material?

CLIO. Let's not be persnickety.

EUTERPE. It *does* matter.

POLYHYMNIA. Wood, surely.

> (AESOP *nods, then places one end of the rod in the hole in the board. He begins to spin the rod with his hands, blowing on it.*)

CLIO. Aha!

MELPOMENE. Making fire with friction!

EUTERPE. Primitive but effective.

URANIA. Certainly less anachronistic.

CALLIOPE. He's a regular *Homo habilis.*

ERATO. Except cuter.

THALIA. I beg to differ.

TERPSICHORE. So do I.

> (AESOP *lifts the stick out of its hole and turns it upside down. He waves his hands and wiggles his fingers over the stick, indicating a glow.*)

CLIO. A flame at last!

(AESOP *uses the lighted stick to look around himself.*)

MELPOMENE. And now he can peer into the darkness.

TERPSICHORE. Thus shines a tiny light in a dark world.

ERATO. A veritable emblem of the human condition.

THALIA. Indeed, humans do have their epistemological limitations.

CALLIOPE. For that matter, so do deities.

EUTERPE. A valid point for all sentient beings.

POLYHYMNIA. But he'd better be careful.

CALLIOPE. The fire is burning lower on the stick.

THALIA. He's liable to get …

(AESOP *suddenly throws his hand up in the air with a silent outcry of pain.*)

MUSES *(together)*. … burned!

(AESOP *waves his hand about frantically.*)

URANIA. Oh, dear.

EUTERPE. His hand is on fire.

(AESOP *waves his entire arm.*)

ERATO. His arm is on fire.

>(AESOP *flails his whole body about, running in circles.*)

TERPSICHORE. He's *all* on fire!

MELPOMENE. He's not going to put it out thrashing about like that.

CLIO. He's only fanning the flames.

MELPOMENE. Somebody should throw a garment over him.

POLYHYMNIA. Or some dirt.

ERATO. I will.

EUTERPE. Don't even think of it.

CALLIOPE. We mustn't interfere.

TERPSICHORE. It's his story.

>(AESOP *throws himself on the ground and writhes about desperately.*)

URANIA. He's covered with third-degree burns by now.

CLIO. Quite hopeless …

ERATO. … even if he could stop the flames.

EUTERPE. No balm in the world will save him.

(AESOP *shrivels himself into a tiny ball and becomes motionless.*)

MELPOMENE. Now he's nothing but a pile of ashes.

POLYHYMNIA. Cremated alive!

TERPSICHORE. How ghastly!

THALIA. Well. His story has clearly reached its dreadful denouement.

URANIA. There's no more to tell.

CLIO. Quite tragic, when you think about it.

MELPOMENE. Not at all. Tragedy is ultimately affirmative.

CALLIOPE. And there's no affirmation here.

POLYHYMNIA. It's altogether pessimistic.

EUTERPE. Nihilistic, I would even say.

CLIO. I don't much care for nihilism. I mean, what's the point of it?

(AESOP *begins to move slightly.*)

URANIA. But behold! Though reduced to a pile of smoldering debris, yet he stirs!

MELPOMENE. There's life in the creature yet.

(AESOP *rises slowly to his feet, pantomiming that his arms have become wings.*)

THALIA. Some metamorphosis has taken place ...

TERPSICHORE. ... a transfiguration into a new phase ...

CLIO. ... a new life cycle ...

CALLIOPE. ... a new instar.

> (AESOP *begins to flap his wings. During the following dialogue, he moves about the stage in pantomimed flight.*)

POLYHYMNIA. Ah, I get it now—the celebrated Phoenix!

THALIA. That's right—rising from the ashes in which he perished!

CALLIOPE. Behold, how this newborn prodigy takes to the air!

URANIA. His sinewy wings doing his wondrous bidding ...

EUTERPE. ... now beating and surging to drive himself onward ...

ERATO. ... now extending in motionless hawk-like majesty ...

TERPSICHORE. ... harnessing a thermal column to lift him yet higher above the gross and paltry earth!

MELPOMENE. And yet—whither is he bound?

CLIO. Ay, that's the question.

CALLIOPE. Whither goes the Phoenix, according to legend?

POLYHYMNIA. I'm not sure the legend even says anything about whither.

EUTERPE. So much fuss about the big bird's fiery death and rebirth …

URANIA. … and nothing at all about what he does in life!

ERATO. Silly legend.

THALIA. And yet, how compelling is this ugly fellow's pantomime!

TERPSICHORE. Indeed.

EUTERPE. Observe how skillfully he weaves into his tale all of the natural elements.

URANIA. That's right …

THALIA. … earth …

ERATO. … water …

POLYHYMNIA. … fire …

MELPOMENE. … air …

POLYHYMNIA. … and all 113 others!

MNEMOSYNE. Oh, enough of this blithering flapdoodle!

CLIO. Don't you like it?

URANIA. I'm quite impressed.

CLIO. Me too.

MELPOMENE. Granted, his theme is elusive.

TERPSICHORE. Surely it's not man's inhumanity to man.

ERATO. Hardly, since he's the only man in the story.

EUTERPE. And he's not even that anymore.

URANIA. Man's inhumanity to himself, then.

THALIA. Of course!

CALLIOPE. Self-abuse!

POLYHYMNIA. An autoerotic allegory!

MELPOMENE. Don't you see, Mother?

CLIO. It's all a matter of interpretation.

MNEMOSYNE. Bother interpretation. I'm against it. A story
is what it is what it is, or it isn't what it isn't what it isn't. No
matter what your definition of "is" is, this story is a clear
case of an isn't. (to AESOP) No more of this inane and
insane dumb show!

(AESOP *continues to pantomime flying.*)

MNEMOSYNE. Cease and desist at once!

(AESOP *continues, moving around the group and
the stage in ever wider circles.*)

MNEMOSYNE. I command you!

CLIO. It's no use, Mother.

URANIA. He turns and turns in the widening gyre.

EUTERPE. He can't even hear you.

MELPOMENE. The center cannot hold.

CALLIOPE. Mere anarchy is loosed upon the world.

MELPOMENE. The blood-dimmed tide is loosed.

CALLIOPE. Everywhere the ceremony of innocence is
    drowned.

THALIA. Let's not exaggerate.

TERPSICHORE. It's only a story.

MELPOMENE. All the same, he *is* all full of passionate
    intensity.

CALLIOPE. There's no denying that.

MNEMOSYNE. But what shall I do now?

CLIO. I surely don't know.

EUTERPE. Nor do I.

ERATO. Nor do any of the rest of us, I fancy.

POLYHYMNIA. Whoever heard of an incantation for stopping a mute and wayward fabulist from pretending he's the Phoenix?

MNEMOSYNE. Well—sometimes one simply must improvise.
 (Raising her arms toward AESOP)
Let these words work as a potion—
Elixir, tonic, brew, or lotion:
No more flailing, no more motion;
No feignèd flight o'er land or ocean.
I'm owed some duty and devotion,
So put an end to this commotion.
Use words instead—a better notion!

 (AESOP *abruptly stops his flight. He staggers for a moment, as if stricken by a sharp blow. Then he gasps and speaks.)*

AESOP. Ah! Ah! Ah! A throat that groans and sighs, lips that shape its noises, a tongue that wags words into shape, great crevasses in my head and chest to echo forth my utterances to all the world! I can speak! I can speak! I can speak!

 (*Silence; the characters freeze and the lights fade as the second act ends.)*

ACT III

(The same; the action is continuous, with all the characters where they were at the end of Act II.)

CLIO *(to* AESOP*).* So—you can speak.

*(*AESOP *nods.)*

EUTERPE. Well, then—what did you want to tell us?

AESOP. Tell you?

POLYHYMNIA. With that bizarre charade of yours.

AESOP. Oh, that. Nothing.

ERATO. Nothing?

AESOP. Nothing.

CALLIOPE. Nothing will come of nothing.

AESOP. To the contrary, *everything* comes of nothing. I just wanted to have my voice.

TERPSICHORE. So you tricked us into giving it to you.

AESOP. Exactly.

THALIA. But don't you have anything to say?

AESOP. Nobody ever does.

MELPOMENE. Well, that *is* rather ... what's the word?

URANIA. True.

CLIO. But also peculiar.

POLYHYMNIA. Awkward.

CALLIOPE. Narratively clumsy.

TERPSICHORE. Disappointing, even.

THALIA *(to* MNEMOSYNE). I told you to steer clear of the ugly ones.

MNEMOSYNE. As myths go, this one *is* unfolding in a most irregular way. I've called a hero; but whether he's accepted or rejected the call, or even whether I've called him to anything in particular—it all seems vague.

EUTERPE. Not your best work.

MNEMOSYNE. No, I should have planned better. Even so, daughters, help me see the thing through. Next, O Homely One, we're supposed to give you amulets or talismans or charms or weapons to use against—well, whatever dragon or demon or monster you're destined to fight in your quest for something-or-other. I do hope there's *some* nemesis awaiting you out there.

AESOP. A pretty trinket, then? I'd love something to wear around my neck—something sparkly.

MNEMOSYNE. Sorry, nothing like that. The only gifts my daughters and I have to offer are those of mind and spirit.

AESOP. Intangible hogwash?

EUTERPE. Depends on how you look at it.

MNEMOSYNE.
>   I offer everything my name implies:
>   Through me, the past is more than just surmise.
>   My gift of memory will etch on your brain
>   Each moment of your life—delight or pain.

CLIO.
>   I, Clio, grant a gift akin to Mother's,
>   And yet it is quite different from all others:
>   To see the human past, as 'twere above it;
>   That's history—or what there's so far of it.

URANIA.
>   And I, Urania, grant you the stars—
>   Knowledge of how they presage peace and wars.
>   You'll have no need for sacred text or scripture,
>   For in your mind, you'll grasp the cosmic picture.

MELPOMENE.
>   Melpomene's my name; in you I'd fashion
>   A heart that's large and open to compassion.
>   The wisdom that I grant is hard but real:
>   Life is a tragedy to those who feel.

THALIA.
>   That's good, sister—but not enough, I fear;
>   A laughing heart is useful, too, and dear.
>   I, Thalia, grant this insight with a wink:
>   Life is a comedy to those who think.

TERPSICHORE.

    A comedy—that's true. And when you laugh,
    Laugh wholly and not shyly, not by half.
    Terpsichore am I, and I'll entrance
    Your lazy feet to cackle and to dance.

CALLIOPE.

    And yet, there is a need for solemn tales,
    And grand ones; I, Calliope, lend sails
    To those who'd steer upon the epic seas,
    Singing of heroes with gracefulness and ease.

ERATO.

    Ah, but what about love? The whole world loves
    A singer who, with choruses of doves,
    Coos, croons, and warbles amatory songs.
    Erato grants you devotees by throngs.

POLYHYMNIA.

    Love? That's nice—if I knew that word's true sense.
    I, Polyhymnia, inspire reverence:
    Prowess with hymns, the power to shape and phrase
        them.
    Believe in gods or not, you still must praise them.

EUTERPE.

    But all these things are nothing more than shallow
    If you do not yourself revere and hallow.
    I, Euterpe, grant you the lyric gift
    To stir your heart, to give it wing and lift.

MNEMOSYNE.

    Well, there you are: nine gifts—no, not nine, ten.
    We don't grant these to ordinary men;
    You've proven yourself special on this day—
    Although we still don't quite know in what way.

AESOP. You're kind and generous. But I ask only for the use of my tongue.

MNEMOSYNE. We've already given you that.

AESOP. Then don't take it away.

CLIO. We never meant to.

MELPOMENE. It's such a trifle.

TERPSICHORE. What about the rest of our gifts?

ERATO. You may have any of them.

EUTERPE. You may have all of them.

AESOP. I've already found them in the silence of my heart.

URANIA. What will you do with them, now that you may speak?

AESOP. I'll lie.

THALIA. Lie!

AESOP. Fib, fudge, falsify, and fabricate. Lie like a rug so vast, it covers the earth and smothers it whole.

CALLIOPE. Worthless scoundrel!

AESOP. You do me too much honor.

POLYHYMNIA. We've unleashed in you eternal wisdom, and this is what you'd do with it?

AESOP. I'll tell the truth.

EUTERPE. You just said you'd lie.

AESOP. The truth is, the world is nothing but lies. Mortal souls invented you gods and goddesses—you were never anything but their lies. Then you created the world and everything in it, including the mortal souls who invented *you*—for they are nothing but *your* lies. It's all a great circle of mendacity, you see. I'll speak, and the parcel of lies that makes up all creation will untie itself and fly to pieces.

CALLIOPE. Excellent.

CLIO. Just the sort of harbinger we relish.

ERATO. A scourge to gods and mortals.

EUTERPE. A living destroyer of all that is.

MELPOMENE. Surely you'll accept just one more gift— outward beauty.

AESOP. I wear my beauty on my soul—which is to say, nowhere.

POLYHYMNIA. You are wise.

TERPSICHORE. You are foolish.

MNEMOSYNE. We are well pleased with you. You may go now—a free man.

AESOP. Sly ones! You'd trick me into accepting the gift I want least! No, I'll go as I came—a slave.

POLYHYMNIA. But why?

AESOP. Why ask me? You are goddesses, all, and you know everything there is to know. What is a master? What is a slave?

CALLIOPE. You tell us, eloquent mortal.

AESOP *(holding out his left hand)*. Behold, ladies, this left hand of mine. It happens to be attached at the moment. It often goes off on its own, and I don't see it for weeks, like some tomcat who thinks only of his belly and scrotum. Not to be trusted with any urgent task. *(Waving his right forefinger scoldingly at his left hand)* Naughty creature! I've got half a mind to hack you off!

> *(His left hand leaps at his throat.)*

AESOP. Ack! Arg! Ech! Rebelling again, traitor? Right hand, to my rescue! Save me from myself!

> *(His right hand grabs his left wrist, grapples with it, and successfully pushes his left hand down to his side, where it hangs limply.)*

AESOP. Another hairbreadth escape! *(Again pointing at his left hand with his right forefinger)* Stay, fiend, or suffer the consequences!

> *(He holds his right hand toward the MUSES.)*

AESOP. Ah, but *this* hand is a loyal fellow, does everything I tell it to. *(To the hand)* Grope this pretty priestess, will you?

> *(He reaches for the PRIESTESS. She cringes and leans away.)*

AESOP *(to his right hand)*. Never mind—she appears to
be ever so slightly on the chaste side. *(To the* MUSES,
displaying his right hand) Why, this good appendage would
throw itself into a burning fire, under a falling ax blade,
beneath the iron-rimmed wheels of a fully loaded ox cart
if I told it to. It's grown hard and callused in my service.
For this hand, you see, is my slave, and I'm its master.
But where is the boundary between slave and master? My
wrist? My elbow? My shoulder? Nay, they do my bidding
too, more or less, so far as they're able. Slaves of mine, all of
them. So where, where is the master I call *me?* Somewhere
in my belly, I imagine, for that's where my best thoughts
come from. Deep down in my wet, smelly entrails, at the
far end of a twisted scheme of levers, wheels, and pulleys—
that's where the master lives. A tiny homunculus, no
doubt, who pulls the strings, who gives commands. But he
must have limbs, too, mustn't he, to pull those strings? A
loyal right hand, at least. And that hand is a slave whom
he must command somehow. So somewhere deep inside
him—perhaps, unlikely as it may seem, in the vile gray
sludge of his brain—resides yet another homunculus. And
so on, deeper and deeper, smaller and smaller—homunculi
within homunculi within homunculi, into the infinite
recesses of minuteness. Tell me—have I got it right?

MNEMOSYNE. There are no such homunculi.

AESOP. Then there can be no masters. And without masters,
how can there be slaves? *(To his right hand)* Don't imagine
this emancipates you, friend. There is no freedom, there
is no tyranny. For do you suppose your fingers are your
slaves? No, because you have no will. Neither do I. Neither
does anybody.

THALIA. Clever.

MELPOMENE. And true.

EUTERPE. But how can you be a slave when there is no such thing?

AESOP. It's a matter of choosing one's imposture. He who pretends to be master lies to himself. He who pretends to be slave lies to the world. Which would *you* choose?

ERATO. Why, he's perfection itself!

URANIA. Beyond perfection!

EUTERPE. Oh, Mother, dear, you did it!

POLYHYMNIA. You did it!

CALLIOPE. You did it!

THALIA. You said that you would do it …

MELPOMENE. … and indeed you did!

URANIA. But still you must admit it …

CLIO. … although you neatly hid it …

URANIA. … you very nearly shitted …

ERATO. … from a case of nerves.

MNEMOSYNE. Oh, maybe for the first three minutes. But after I saw that I had it licked hands down, it was a dreadful bore. Never again for me, I tell you. No more ugly slave mute mimes transformed into agents of apocalyptic destruction. The whole thing has been like a vacation in the Underworld. Thank Whatever-Powers-May-Be it's over. And if this fellow fulfills his potential and unravels the fabric of the cosmos itself, that pretty well assures my retirement, doesn't it? Complete oblivion—that *is* a consummation devoutly to be wished. Best for everybody, I'm sure. And now, daughters, thank you for your help. I could have managed without you, but it was nice doing a little something as a family after all these centuries. Now you must hurry back to work, save the damned human race from its evolutionary ineptitude. A hopeless cause, no doubt, but there *is* something to be said for futile gestures.

CLIO. Right-o.

EUTERPE. We're off.

ERATO *(patting* AESOP *on the cheek).* And now that you've got your voice, adorable fellow, do try to make the best use of it.

AESOP. No chance of that.

ERATO. No, I suppose not. "Do as thou wilt"—that's better advice. 'Bye, now. I don't suppose we'll meet again. A pity. We'll never know what might have been between us.

MELPOMENE. Oh, for pity's sake.

THALIA. Enough of this vulgar flirtation.

CLIO. *Do* stop throwing yourself at the creature.

POLYHYMNIA. Let's bustle.

TERPSICHORE. There's work to do.

(One by one, the NINE MUSES *exit into
the tree—*CLIO, URANIA, MELPOMENE,
THALIA, TERPSICHORE, CALLIOPE, ERATO,
POLYHYMNIA, *and* EUTERPE.)

CLIO.
　　Exit Muses …

URANIA.
　　　　　　… now that we're done …

MELPOMENE.
　　… With all the work …

THALIA.
　　　　　　… we had begun.

TERPSICHORE.
　　We must hurry …

CALLIOPE.
　　　　　　… we must run …

ERATO.
　　… Sacred sisters …

POLYHYMNIA.
　　　　　　… one by one …

EUTERPE.
　　… Promptly, quickly …

MUSES *(together)*.
　　　　　　… till all are gone!

(The tree still stands open. AESOP, MNEMOSYNE, *and the* PRIESTESS *are left alone onstage—the latter still staring in awestruck muteness from the bench.* MNEMOSYNE *approaches* AESOP.*)*

MNEMOSYNE.

    How very odd!
I came your destiny to show you;
Prodigious powers now overflow you.
Are you my debtor? Do I owe you?
Now that we're done, I still don't know you.
    How very odd!
Through all that's happened since I came
I've still not even learned your name.

AESOP.

    I'll tell you; it's—

MNEMOSYNE.

             Don't—'twould be a shame;
For I'll forget, my brain's so lame.
    It must seem odd
That I, Goddess of Memory,
Shall henceforth disremember thee.
Oh, how I hope you'll pardon me!
You may well ask …

AESOP.

              How can that be?

MNEMOSYNE.

    It's not so odd;
For memory, that brain sensation
Of which I am the incarnation—
Yea, the matrix and foundation—

Is nothing but imagination.
    No, not so odd;
Memory of our world, our stage, is
But a tale of fools and sages,
Turning ever forth by pages
On and on for countless ages.
    No, not so odd,
For there's no memory at all—
Just stories from a crystal ball
That falsely claims it can recall
All things past, both great and small.
    No, not so odd,
Nor always false—for just by chance—
Ay, solely due to happenstance—
A story told may somehow glance
Some truth amid wild falsehood's dance.
    Now *here's* what's odd:
The time for memory is through,
And my life's validation too.
All that's to come I leave to you.
Until forever—toodle-oo.

AESOP. Toodle-oo to you, sweet phantom goddess.

    (MNEMOSYNE *walks toward the open tree;*
    THALIA *peeks out.*)

THALIA. Oh, Mother, dear …

MNEMOSYNE. What do *you* want?

THALIA. Don't forget to switch the Priestess back on before
    you lock up.

MNEMOSYNE (*looking at the* PRIESTESS). Oh, bother.

THALIA. Do I need to tell you the incantation for release?

MNEMOSYNE. No. Be on your way.

THALIA. I can wait.

MNEMOSYNE. You don't trust your own mother?

THALIA. Oh, how can you ask? No.

MNEMOSYNE. Here it is, then. *(Turning toward the* PRIESTESS *and holding out her arms)* Rise. Speak.

> *(Released from her spell, the* PRIESTESS *leaps up from the bench and throws herself on her knees before* MNEMOSYNE.*)*

PRIESTESS. Forgive my blasphemy, Divine One!

MNEMOSYNE *(to* THALIA*)*. Now look what you made me do.

THALIA. Right. All's well. Ta, then.

> (THALIA *disappears into the tree.*)

PRIESTESS. I believe in you, Mnemosyne, Bringer of Memory! Help my unbelief!

MNEMOSYNE. Didn't I just tell you to rise? You can't get the simplest thing right. I wash my hands of you.

> (MNEMOSYNE *turns to go.*)

PRIESTESS. Don't go, Sweet Goddess!

MNEMOSYNE. Giving me orders now, are you?

PRIESTESS. Hear my prayer!

MNEMOSYNE. A prayer is nothing but a mortal's way of bossing gods around.

PRIESTESS. Let me follow you and worship you.

MNEMOSYNE. Follow me the tiniest fraction of an inch and I'll smite you yet.

PRIESTESS. Don't you wish to be worshipped?

MNEMOSYNE. Yes, I do have a certain vanity that way. But I prefer to be worshipped unobtrusively, from afar. I like my space. A great gulf fixed—that's what I try to keep between me and my worshippers. And now I'm off to my side of the gulf.

(MNEMOSYNE *turns to go.*)

PRIESTESS. But sweet Goddess, you leave me baffled and bereft of purpose.

MNEMOSYNE. How nice to know I've not lost my touch.

PRIESTESS. Tell me, I implore you—what is my sacred duty?

MNEMOSYNE. Worm! How dare you aspire to sacred duty? Leave sacredness to the gods.

PRIESTESS. But—what am I to do?

MNEMOSYNE. Since when do deities tell mortals what to do? We're more inclined toward "thou-shalt-*not*" sorts of commands. Thou shalt not do this, thou shalt not do that.

PRIESTESS. Then what shall I *not* do?

MNEMOSYNE. Don't believe.

PRIESTESS. Believe what?

MNEMOSYNE. Anything.

PRIESTESS. Not even all that I've just seen with my own eyes?

MNEMOSYNE. That least of all.

PRIESTESS. But—

MNEMOSYNE. Not another word.

PRIESTESS. But—

MNEMOSYNE. We can do this the easy way or the hard way.

PRIESTESS. But—

MNEMOSYNE. All right, then, I'll lay down the law. Don't worship me. Not obtrusively, unobtrusively, from afar, or anywhere.

PRIESTESS. But—

MNEMOSYNE. Better yet, don't worship anybody. I wouldn't wish your devotion on the nastiest deity in the most beastly pantheon ever devised. Your adoration is more obnoxious than your blasphemy. Poor Isis—the trouble you must have given whomever-she-is.

PRIESTESS. But—

MNEMOSYNE. Do you wish to be smote?

PRIESTESS. No.

MNEMOSYNE. Obey me, then. Or don't. Just leave me alone.

>(*The* PRIESTESS *sits;* MNEMOSYNE *turns toward* AESOP.)

MNEMOSYNE. But *you*—I believe I know you from somewhere, do I not?

>(AESOP *shrugs.*)

MNEMOSYNE. I do, I'm sure of it. What's your name, homely fellow?

>(AESOP *shrugs.*)

MNEMOSYNE. Don't you know?

>(AESOP *nods.*)

MNEMOSYNE. Then why don't you tell me?

>(*Again,* AESOP *reaches inside his mouth, pulls out his tongue by its tip with his fingers, and lets go of it. It falls limply to his chin. He takes hold of it with his fingers again, rolls it up, and stuffs it back inside his mouth.*)

MNEMOSYNE. Oh. You are mute.

(AESOP *nods.*)

MNEMOSYNE. Forgive me. I took you for someone eloquent.

(MNEMOSYNE *turns toward the* PRIESTESS.)

MNEMOSYNE. And *you*—well, I'm sure we've never met, and my instinct tells me it's just as well.

> (*The stage darkens; low thunder and lightning;* MNEMOSYNE *falls silent for a moment, then speaks to herself.*)

MNEMOSYNE.
    But what about me?
    How can this be?
My own acquaintance I've not made.
    What is my name?
    It seems a shame;
My mind is going, I'm afraid.
    My lines I forget,
    But I'll not fret:
My role I have already played.
    And now this tree
    Calls me to flee
Into the stupor of its shade.

> (*The stage darkens further as* MNEMOSYNE *walks into the open tree; a loud crack of thunder as the tree shuts behind her. Then silence, and the lights rise again—not an unearthly golden glow, but the bland and banal sunlight of an earthly afternoon.* AESOP *resumes digging. The* PRIESTESS *rises from the bench and talks to herself dazedly.*)

PRIESTESS. Surely I have had a most rare vision. I have had a dream, past the wit of woman to say what dream it was. The eye of woman has not heard, the ear of woman has not seen, woman's hand is not able to taste, her ear to conceive, nor her heart to report … Oh, such disordering of the senses!

(She stares at AESOP *for a moment.)*

PRIESTESS. Pardon me, good fellow.

(AESOP *stops digging and looks at her.)*

PRIESTESS. Can you speak?

AESOP. No.

PRIESTESS. Oh.

(She turns away, then turns toward him again.)

PRIESTESS. Oh!

(AESOP *solemnly drops to his knees.)*

AESOP. By what name shall I address you, dreaded destroyer of trees? What epithet most honors and suits you? All-covering Hela, goddess of the realm of shadows? Infant-slain Mictecacihuatl, watcher over the bones of the dead? Night-woman Hine-nui-te-po, for whom the fantail wakes and laughs? Triple-natured Morrigan, dark hovering bird of battlefields? Violent Ereshkigal, sky-sister abducted by the depths? Withering Morana, dark and frosty daughter of the sun? Incubus-wedded Santa Muerte, tequila-guzzling bearer of roses by bunches?

PRIESTESS. You mock me.

AESOP. Always and faithfully.

PRIESTESS. Arise—and let us say our farewells.

AESOP. So—what will you do now?

PRIESTESS. You who are wise-foolish and foolish-wise, surely
you know already.

AESOP. You'll continue your mission.

PRIESTESS. Yes.

AESOP. You can't heal or raise from the dead. But you can
comfort and destroy. When the only comfort is death,
you'll grant it.

PRIESTESS. I'll never slay another living soul.

AESOP. No one can live without destroying life. Even fruit
must be plucked and slain to be eaten.

PRIESTESS. I'll live.

AESOP. Without a miracle? You no longer believe.

PRIESTESS. Who says so?

AESOP. The Muses.

PRIESTESS. Shall I be commanded by goddesses who tell me
they don't exist?

AESOP. So what *do* you believe in? Not Isis, surely.

PRIESTESS (*picking up her fallen stole, wiping the spit off it with her sleeve, and placing it again on her shoulders*). True, not her. But not one jot or tittle of my purpose shall pass from my calling—to spread worship of the goddess throughout the world. People can be made to believe in her, but *not* in the spirit that truly spurs me on—the spirit of You.

AESOP. Me?

PRIESTESS (*laughing*). Not *you*—or not *merely* you. The sacred You.

AESOP. Ah. The *You* that is all others.

PRIESTESS. All things that live.

AESOP. For *You* is their one true name.

PRIESTESS. Yes.

AESOP.
  You …

PRIESTESS.
  … Is the mantra of mantras,
  The talisman word.

AESOP.
  You …

PRIESTESS.
  … Is the sacred text
  Not to be uttered backward,
  For that is the way of hate.

AESOP.
>You …

PRIESTESS.
>… Is the space between voices,
>The measure of that space,
>The bridge across.

AESOP.
>You …

PRIESTESS.
>… Is the blade that severs,
>The needle and thread that mend,
>The gasp of delight,
>The ache.

AESOP. Compassion, then—the vilest profanation against the gods.

PRIESTESS. For it comes from the heart, and nowhere else.

AESOP. I'm sorry for you. Whom the gods would destroy, they first inspire to love.

PRIESTESS. As long as I disguise myself with the mask of a priestess, I can do my sacred work.

AESOP. You'll be found out someday—and shunned, and reviled.

PRIESTESS. And slain. Nailed to such a tree as this. But till then, till then … *(Pause)* Why did you bless me?

AESOP. *I blessed you?*

PRIESTESS. You made me witness to your story. Why?

AESOP. You were the first living soul who didn't take one look at me and call me ugly.

PRIESTESS. I thought it.

AESOP. You didn't say it.

PRIESTESS. I needed your help.

AESOP. So. You'd have said I was ugly if you didn't have other things on your mind?

PRIESTESS. Yes.

AESOP. Liar.

PRIESTESS. Tell me.

AESOP. I needed someone with faith. I've got no faith of my own.

PRIESTESS. Not true. You had faith that I'd have faith. Hush, let's stop, now that I've bested you. We'll meet again. I have faith in it. *(Looking around)* Oh—which way is it to the highway?

AESOP *(pointing right)*. That way.

PRIESTESS *(with a broad smile)*. Thank you, my friend.

> *(The* PRIESTESS *exits in the opposite direction— to the left. After a pause,* AESOP *speaks to the audience.)*

AESOP.
> I am alone—or so I say
>> Because I am supposed to;
> You know the truth is not a thing
>> I'm really quite disposed to.
> And flights of verse treat facts much worse
>> Than statements spoke in prose do.
>
> "I am alone": Let it be known,
>> I find those words most queer.
> For I am standing on a stage,
>> Addressing you loud and clear,
> While you are sitting in your chairs
>> Pretending you're not here.
>
> I am alone, I am alone,
>> Standing at stage center,
> Awaiting someone who may be
>> My savior or tormentor—
> Waiting, waiting, nothing more,
>> For someone else to enter.
>
> I am alone; watch closely now—
>> Yes, you and all your chums—
> This tap-tap-tapping of my toes,
>> This twiddling of my thumbs.
> My tongue I'll click, my nose I'll pick,
>> Till something this way comes.
>
> I am alone; so seize this time
>> (It really would be wise)
> To hold each other by the hand,
>> To stroke each others' thighs,
> Or gaze and gaze, entranced, amazed,
>> Into each others' eyes.

I am alone; now aren't I
  A fascinating sight?
For you can't look away from me;
  Tell me if I'm not right.
For you can't look away from me;
  Try it with all your might.

I am alone and wear a mask,
  Just as all actors should.
And yet—I touch my face and feel
  That it is flesh and blood.
Now touch *your* frozen face—you'll find
  It's linen, cork, or wood.

"I am alone": These words have spun
  A gripping spell, it's true;
Moments are passing, lost and gone—
  Moments that you shall rue;
For when you peep in a play too deep,
  The play peeps into you.

(Pause; then the STEWARD *enters.)*

STEWARD. Ah, I catch you loafing, do I? I won't beat you this
  time. Nay, I'll not beat you any time, never again, for the
  worst has happened. Well, not the worst, I suppose, for I
  still live and breathe and have tomorrow to look forward
  to, at least hypothetically. But the same may not be said for
  you—not with any reliability.

  (AESOP *looks at him impassively and silently.)*

STEWARD. But by all the gods, a little silence, please! You'll
  do yourself no good with all these shrill and hysterical
  questions, one piling upon the next, poking and porking

and scrogging and buggering away at one another in a deafening concupiscent heap of obscene moaning and caterwauling. No, no good at all. Silence! I demand it!

There. That's better.

Now let me collect my thoughts. For I've got serious thinking to do, even if *your* days of thinking—if you ever had any—are over, and your sorrows and joys as well.

"What's the matter?" you ask, more calmly now—and a reasonable question it is.

"The master is the matter," I reply.

"What?" you ask. "Is he no longer the idiot he was?"

Oh, certainly, for there's no cure for idiocy except getting off one's lower bodily stratum and putting one's native intelligence to use, of which he is unable, or at least unwilling. Nevertheless, our interview did not unfold in its customary manner, for his repulsive wife and his decrepit daughters were present, uncharacteristically concerned about the state of the estate and nagging and fretting most fearfully about every detail.

As always, the master asked me for a full account of what all his slaves are doing. I told him all—or almost all, hoping as always that he'd forget about you.

But he did not forget about you, for he never does.

"What is the ugly mute one doing?" he asked.

And I told him, as I always do, "I've got him digging holes."

And he asked, as he always does, "Why is he digging holes?"

And I replied, as I always do, "So he may fill them later."

But before he could utter his ever-satisfied "oh," his frightful excuse for a wife piped up.

"That's no purpose," she squawked.

"No, no purpose at all," echoed his daughters in shrill unison, like the trio of unholy harpies they veritably are.

And the master, too apathetic with stupidity and horniness to argue, sauntered off to the meadow where dwell his woolly paramours, leaving the matter in the all-too-capable hands of the household's distaff deputation.

And the wife and daughters gave me orders to take you at once to the village and sell you at auction there. We must hurry, for the bidding begins at once.

(Pause)

STEWARD. So my tidings have stunned you into silence, eh? That's just as well, for I have trouble enough on my hands. Mine is now the onerous duty to get a good price for you. If I bring the master a pittance, he'll dock my pay—or at least his hideous women will. But what can I sell you for, since you've got no value I can imagine? As scrap, I suppose. To be slaughtered and chopped up for one use or another. What use might that be? Not enough lime in your flesh to use as mortar. You're too wet for kindling or fuel—your fat would sizzle no matter how long it was left out to dry. I don't know what your meat would taste like, but you don't look any too appetizing. Oh, I've got it! Compost! Yes, your carcass will make most excellent manure—except for your bones, but a kennel of dogs could get a week's tasty merriment out of them.

(The STEWARD turns to go, laughing as he speaks.)

STEWARD. Come along—and no talking back, now.

AESOP *(not moving)*. Of course not.

(The STEWARD stops in his tracks and turns slowly toward AESOP.)

STEWARD. What was that?

AESOP. No talking back. Absolutely not.

STEWARD. You can speak?

AESOP. So it would seem.

STEWARD. I don't much like this. I don't like this at all.

AESOP. Don't worry. I can't hear.

STEWARD. Blind too, I suppose.

AESOP. Utterly senseless. I cannot see or hear or touch or smell or taste anything that doesn't come crawling on all fours out of my imagination.

STEWARD. How long have you been able to talk?

AESOP. I don't know. I never tried before.

STEWARD. Willfully silent all these years?

AESOP. Who can say?

STEWARD. Well, this won't do, don't you see? You were useless before, but now you're worse than useless. Who'll buy some unsightly monster who spouts nonsense? I won't even be able to pay someone to take you off my hands.

AESOP. Gag me.

STEWARD. Yes, and while I'm at it, I'll hang a sign around your neck that says, "This one talks too much."

AESOP. Cut out my tongue.

STEWARD. And try to get a good price for you freshly
maimed? You're full of fine ideas. No, you're unsellable,
that's all. I've got no choice but to take you straight to the
master and tell him—

AESOP. Yes, the master—he who likes to fornicate with sheep
because his wife is too ugly and his daughters too old.

STEWARD. Merciful Artemis! Would you really go repeating
such things? No. You'd get me beaten and fired, but you'd
get yourself killed, be sure of that. Now see here—you'll
go with me to auction right now, and I'll forget you ever
spoke, and I'll say you're mute, and you won't say a word.
Do you promise?

AESOP. How can anyone promise anything? We know
nothing of what's to be—not even our coming forth or
going thither. My only answer must be "yes" and "no."

STEWARD. Which shall it be, then?

AESOP. What do you mean?

STEWARD. Your answer—"yes" or "no"?

AESOP. Both.

(*The* STEWARD *sits brokenly on the bench.*)

STEWARD. How the great wheel has turned. Only an hour
ago, I gave you commands. Now you have the power to
destroy me.

AESOP. Mine is the power to destroy the very fabric of reality.

STEWARD. Boastful as well.

AESOP. Not at all. I'm humility itself. If I destroy the world, who will be first to go? Me, of course. The prospect puts me all a-tremble.

STEWARD. Do it, please. It would relieve my woes.

AESOP. Don't be so dramatic. All will be well. Just humor me a little. Tell me another story about your prophet of love.

STEWARD. He's not *my* prophet.

AESOP. Then who else can tell me his stories?

STEWARD. No one. And it's best that way. You've heard too much already. Now that you can talk, you'll blab to everyone about him.

AESOP. Not so. Now that my tongue is loosed, I have my own tales to tell. I've less power to repeat your words than I did when I was mute.

STEWARD. That makes some kind of sense, I guess.
　　Well, then.
　　Once during the last days of this prophet's life, while he was roaming the land with his followers, word reached him that a dear friend of his—Lazarus, let's call him—was sick in a nearby village. Now, love gave this prophet the power to restore sight to the blind and hearing to the deaf, and to heal the worst sorts of poxes and sores. And yet he delayed in going to Lazarus. His followers wondered why.
　　Then after a time he told them, "We will go now to Lazarus, who is asleep."

"If he's only asleep," they replied, "all he has to do is wake up."

"No," said the prophet, "for his is the sleep of death."

So they went to the village, and found that Lazarus had already been in his tomb for four days.

The prophet wept.

"Remove the stone from the entrance to the tomb," said the prophet.

"No," said Lazarus's family. "For by now, there must be an awful stink inside."

"Do it," commanded the prophet.

And they did it. And the stink inside really was as bad as you can imagine.

"Lazarus, come forth," called the prophet. "In the name of love, come forth."

And Lazarus came forth, still wound in his linen shroud, his face wrapped up as well, smelling as sweet as a lilac.

And the prophet told his followers and Lazarus's family, "Remove those garments of death, and dress him up well and proper. He and I and all the rest of you will feast together."

(Pause)

AESOP. Where did you hear such stories?

STEWARD. They just come to me. This one came to me just now.

AESOP. So you make them up.

STEWARD. If you say so.

AESOP. Your stories are true. They just haven't happened yet.

STEWARD. Why do I believe you?

AESOP. Because you are a fool.

    (Pause)

STEWARD. No. I *don't* believe you. My stories make no
sense—this one least of all. "The prophet wept," I said. Now
why would he weep? He knew that he would raise Lazarus
from the dead. He had nothing to be sad about.

AESOP. He wept because he knew there is no such thing as
death. He longed for death to release him from the eternal
pain of love.

STEWARD. You have become wise.

AESOP. I am as much a fool as you.

STEWARD. A fool who can fool folks into thinking yourself
wise. *(Snapping his finger)* Yes, that's it! I'll sell you as a
tutor! Why, your very ugliness will be an asset! The uglier,
the smarter—that's what some buyer will think. But not a
word about not being able to read or write.
    You *can't* read or write, can you?
    Good—not that there'd be any harm in it, just one less
alarming alteration in the order of things.
    Just say something clever and judicious to any gullible
rich fellow who seems ready to offer a good price for you.
    You can do that, can't you?
    Good.
    It's settled.
    Come along.

    (As the STEWARD *turns to go, his eyes fall upon the
tree.)*

STEWARD. But by my sacred groin—the tree!

AESOP. What of it?

STEWARD. Just look at it!

AESOP. I'm looking at it.

STEWARD. It's dead!

AESOP. Not so.

STEWARD. Do you think I don't know a dead tree when I see one? It was scattered with a few leaves before, but now it's bare entirely. And its branches—dead and dry enough for firewood. Ass! Did you strike its roots with your shovel? Or—

> (*The* STEWART *turns toward* AESOP *and stares at him.*)

STEWARD. You!

AESOP. Take care how you speak that word.

STEWARD. Who are you?

AESOP. You tell me.

STEWARD. The wanderer who haunts my thoughts with his stories—the prophet of love, the hater of fig trees.

AESOP. No such animal.

STEWARD. You spoke true, then. Your slightest word is destruction.

AESOP. I've destroyed nothing.

STEWARD. The tree is dead.

AESOP. It is asleep.

STEWARD. The sleep of death.

AESOP. There's nothing dead about it.

STEWARD. Nay, I know what you are. You are the whole of divinity itself, taken the shape of man. And there's only one thing to be done with you.

> (*The* STEWARD *lunges at* AESOP, *seizes him by the throat, and slams him against the tree trunk, throttling him and lifting him fully off the ground.*)

STEWARD. I'll slay your temporal husk and send you back to the infinite.

> (AESOP *kicks, gags, and chokes for a few moments; then, his feet still dangling above the ground, he relaxes and breathes easily; he laughs.*)

AESOP. You cannot do it.

STEWARD. Die!

AESOP. You want to destroy love—a worthy purpose. But I am not love. Love is not a thing you can seize by the throat.

STEWARD. Die, whatever you are!

AESOP. Your fingers hang limp around my neck like a dishrag. Were it your will to kill me, I'd be dead.

(Silence; the STEWARD *slowly lets* AESOP *go, then sits on the bench.)*

STEWARD. I have no will.

AESOP. Nor do I.

STEWARD. Yours is the only will there is.

AESOP. Story is the only will. All else is ever in its thrall.

STEWARD. But the tree—

AESOP. Asleep, as I told you. Dormant—not for a season, but for the day.

STEWARD. The day?

AESOP. By night it thrives and blooms—only then.

STEWARD. I don't believe it.

AESOP. Don't. That's always best. But let me show you.

> (AESOP *raises his face and hands to the sky; as he speaks, a tangible deep darkness settles over the stage.)*

AESOP.
  O daylight, bringer forth of naught,
  Ye sunbeams from which nothing's wrought
      But spirits, specters, phantoms, ghosts,
      Unreal multitudes and hosts—
  O daylight flee, set free our thought.

Speed the hours, let time make haste,
By this my rhyming swiftly chased.
    Take with you, daylight, all chimera
    That trick the mind through every era,
Until with darkness we are graced.

Let dusk descend with all that's real;
Let sweet obscurity reveal
    The life that hides behind the light,
    Creation that resides in night;
Yea, nothing from our hearts conceal.

STEWARD. Such darkness as this I have not seen.

AESOP. You're a bit late for your auction.

STEWARD. But this is no night—or no ordinary night. No stars, no moon—and yet no clouds to cover them from sight. Is this promised end?

AESOP. And the promised beginning, and the promised middle.

STEWARD. The heavens themselves have ceased to exist. It is a void.

AESOP. Not void—for void must have space to contain it, time for it to endure. In this night, we have not space or time or void. And although you and I may imagine ourselves chatting, how could that be, for when or where might our words find habitation?

STEWARD. Oh, slave uncanny, servile sorcerer, undo your spell, lift off of me this horror of great darkness.

AESOP. Not darkness, either, since there can be no darkness without its opposite. There is only the Lullaby Tree— timeless, spaceless, silent, nonexistent even itself, and yet all that remains.

STEWARD. Put the world as it was, and then be mute again!

AESOP. I would if you wished it.

STEWARD. I do.

AESOP. No, for you have longed for this moment in your heart of heart of hearts since first you breathed the air. You know it. Your very horror tells you so.

> (Silence)

STEWARD. It's true. And soon I shall join in this timeless, silent, voidless void—body, mind, memories, all! O perfect fulfillment of my desires!

AESOP. Hope betrays you, as hope betrays all. No such fulfillment awaits. For the voidless void is unstable, inherently and always. There is no death—no lasting death. Your prophet knew it. His knowledge made him weep. Story always disturbs nothingness, harasses and torments it, destroys it, wrenches it into somethingness.

STEWARD. Story.

AESOP. Ay, Story—a deeper and more fearful thing than even Love.

> (As AESOP speaks, an explosive glow appears
> below the stage underneath the tree, first in a small

ball, then spreading out among the tree's roots;
instrumental music is heard.)

AESOP.

Behold, beneath our idle toes,
Amid the roots that lay a-doze,
A storied egg has cracked its shell,
Releasing heat as hot as hell.
Time and space now come to be,
Setting sundry forces free,
And primal sparks newborn, untried,
Rush now asunder, now collide.
Creation here begins anew;
Make all paths straight for Sacred You!

(The glow climbs the tree trunk, illuminating it to the
core; music continues.)

AESOP.

Up through the trunk rise crackling saps;
All symmetries must now collapse
As atoms self-create and swarm
And matter takes its storied form.
Things must cohere, and things must break,
At once annihilate and make.
Though what unfolds may now confuse,
Fear not the madness that ensues.
This truth defies what you may think:
Creation comes at chaos' brink.

(The glow spreads through the branches, taking the
shapes of stars and galaxies—blazing blue, white,
yellow, and orange; black tendrils also form around
the trunk and branches; music continues.)

AESOP.

>Amid the branches, then their twigs,
>Clustered all about like figs,
>Bloom gas clouds, stars, and galaxies—
>Storied seething without cease.
>Yet all is not suffused in light;
>For darkness must exert its might
>To nip and pinch and also prune
>Unneeded sun, superfluous moon.
>Dark vines of matter's opposite
>Rein in the arbor lest it split.

>*(Stars and galaxies continue to appear amid the branches; others vanish in bright flashes; music continues.)*

AESOP.

>Ages, eons past all thought
>Rush by us faster than they ought.
>From this vantage we possess,
>We see what mortals seldom guess—
>That storied stars are mortal too.
>When one just born comes into view,
>Another dies—appalling sight—
>Erupting with a searing light
>Until upon itself it crashes,
>Left infinitely black, all ashes.

>*(The evolution of the cosmic tree continues; a chorus of human voices joins the instrumental music.)*

AESOP.

>But listen now—somewhere sing voices.
>An infant sentience rejoices,
>Aware of its own power to strive,

Exulting just to be alive.
Listen, listen, sharp, alert;
Let not your hearing now avert;
This storied singing you must cherish,
For in a twinkling it shall perish;
Life's much more fleeting than a star.
But where think you those voices are?

(AESOP *searches the tree for a moment, then points
to a tiny galaxy, shaped like the Milky Way; music
with voices continues.*)

AESOP.

Ah, here—this meager smudge of light,
So scant it nearly 'scapes our sight.
And yet it's huge beyond all scope,
Exceeding power to yearn and hope:
Some million million stars extending
Toward storied fates beyond portending.
Yes, here, along its fading rim—
Here's raised the song, here's raised the hymn.
And just who may these singers be?
I'll tell you true—they're you and me.

(AESOP *points to a star which has grown especially
large and wobbles on a high branch.*)

AESOP.

But now see there—a star grown ripe;
It looks a most delicious type,
All plump and succulent and sweet,
Now storied just enough to eat.
Its stem shall presently be loosed;
A fall would leave it badly bruised.
Oh, such a star with such a taste

Would be a dreadful thing to waste.
Catch it, catch it! Quick, pursue it!
Catch it, catch it! No, I'll do it!

(AESOP *rushes beneath the star just as it falls from
its branch; he deftly catches it.*)

AESOP.

Oh, but how my heart is beating!
For here I hold it for the eating.
No, do not ask to taste it first;
I'm much too eager, fit to burst.
'Twas I who caught it, and not you;
A storied bite or two's my due.
A star! Such rapt expectancy
I feel at what's in store for me!
The fruit that from this tree has sprung
Is now the captive of my tongue.

(AESOP *tastes the star and closes his eyes as he
speaks; he glows from within.*)

AESOP.

Shut tight, my eyes, so I may savor
This infinitely fruited flavor—
Melting on my tongue the manna
Of the smoothly ripe banana;
And, oh, yes, mulberry too,
Tasting of purple, black, and blue,
While simultaneously I glean
The tartness of the tangerine;
Also the peach, so oft rebuffed
Unjustly for its close-cropped tuft.

(AESOP *takes another bite.*)

AESOP.

> The mango, picked down from its bower;
> Pineapple sweet pressed 'gainst its flower;
> The lemon sour, which can't be known
> Unmixed with taste to ease its own;
> Scarlet cherry, whose smart roundness
> Completes its flavorful profoundness;
> And apples—simplest and best?
> Not, I think, against this test:
> 'Mid all the rest, the taste most big—
> That of the storied, bread-like fig.

> (AESOP *breaks the star open, revealing countless stars inside.)*

AESOP.

> I break wide open this bright planet—
> Behold, it is a pomegranate!
> The kind from which good chutney's made,
> Or juice or sauce or marinade;
> A fruit with seeds lusciously full,
> Each one as splendid as the whole,
> Each one itself a blazing ball.
> It's your turn now—taste all,
> Taste some, taste just a few;
> The storied choice is up to you.

> (AESOP *holds the broken star toward the* STEWARD, *who trembles and takes a few of the shining seeds in his fingers, then tastes them. Like* AESOP, *he suddenly glows from within. He drops to his knees in awe and wonder.)*

STEWARD. Zeus be praised!

AESOP. It's only a story.

>   *(Music and darkness settle over the stage as the play ends.)*